W9-BPJ-440

NEVER ALONE

J. MANOA

EPIC
Escape

An Imprint of EPIC Press
EPICPRESS.COM

Never Alone
Werewolf Council: Book #1

Written by J. Manoa

Copyright © 2018 by Abdo Consulting Group, Inc.

Published by EPIC Press™
PO Box 398166
Minneapolis, MN 55439

All rights reserved.

Printed in the United States of America.

Cover design by Candice Keimig & Neil Klinepier
Images for cover art obtained from iStockPhoto.com
Edited by Ryan Hume

LIBRARY OF CONGRESS CATALOGING-IN-PUBLICATION DATA
Names: Manoa, J., author.
Title: Never alone / by J. Manoa.
Description: Minneapolis, MN : EPIC Press, 2018. | Series: Werewolf council ; #1
Summary: As children, Nathaniel Wallace and Riley McKnight bonded over losing their
    fathers. Years later, they pass their time watching movies and imagining elaborate stories
    about the their small, Alaskan town. But Nate soon learns that his real life is more bizarre
    than any fiction.
Identifiers: LCCN 2016946213 | ISBN 9781680764987 (lib. bdg.)
    | ISBN 9781680765540 (ebook)
Subjects: LCSH: Friendship—Fiction. | Werewolves—Fiction. | Young adult fiction.
Classification: DDC [Fic]—dc23
LC record available at http://lccn.loc.gov/2016946213

EPIC
Press

EPICPRESS.COM

For 예원

PROLOGUE

London, 1882

HER FEET POUNDED THROUGH THE RAINWATER on the cobblestones. Her breathing was a short, panicked rhythm released as puffs of mist. Her legs burned from movement, ached from pushing herself forward through the damp street. Her feet sloshed water behind her, and she nearly slid from every step. She looked behind her quickly, out of instinct, but turned back before losing her balance. The street ahead was bathed in watery light from the lampposts lining the road. The street behind her was the same: rippled footprints showing her pursuers a clear trail. She didn't know where they were, but they were there. They were behind her. Their footsteps lost under the chorus of rain.

A screeching wind cut through the air at her back. Her legs stuck together and she smacked into the road, sliding through the water.

She kicked. A thin wire tugged at her legs just below the knee. It dug into her skin as though moving too much could cause it to slice through. She rolled over to look and could barely see the thin line wrapping around her legs, attached to a pair of metal balls sagging with weight. She'd lost her shoes somewhere in the distance, and as she looked past her bare feet and down the alley, she saw their silhouettes.

"Please," she said between shallow breaths.

Rain cascaded from their black cloaks as though repelled. The nearest of the four hooded figures came to a stop so close that she retracted her feet until the wire dug into her legs. In the dim light, she could see a cloth stretched between the two sides of his hood, covering his nose and mouth. His eyes were nothing but shadow.

"Please," she said again, "I've done nothing."

The figure turned as the other three gathered behind him. They moved into a half-moon around her. "For he does not bear the sword in vain," the central figure said. The shadows of his face turned toward her.

"For he is a servant of God," said another, also a man.

"Please," she panted, hoping they could hear her over the steady drumming of rain. "I've no—no quarrel with you, sirs."

"An avenger who carries out God's wrath on the wrongdoer," the second man continued.

"I desire only peace," she muttered. "Peace for my family." Her words barely escaped her quivering lips. "Peace between our people."

There was a lightning flash. A metal blade extended from the sleeve of his right arm.

Her lungs filled with an intense heat. "Don't," she begged. "Don't make me do this."

Three other blades emerged around her, locking into place with a round of metallic clicks.

She felt herself burning from the inside of her chest. Her muscles twitched as the heat spread through her body. Her lungs, her heart, her bones, her skin, the inside of her eyelids—they were all on fire. She gritted her teeth, shaking even down to their roots.

"Watch what she becomes," said one of them.

She felt her clothes tighten around her limbs. She heard them burst. The wire around her legs dug in before snapping with a loud pop. The rain began to soak through the dense hairs that sprouted out of her skin. She growled, feeling the sound rise as though ripped up from her heart.

The men seemed to disappear. She could sense a thin blue coating of moisture covering the dull gray of stone, the greens and purples and blues of dust and metal, the lingering yellow and orange of horse and human. Cool colors of inorganic scents overwhelmed the warm ones of man and animal, objects propelled by the blood in their veins, streamed like smoke trails.

In front of her, one bright spot shined like a lighthouse through the torrent—some kind of light painted over the leader's hood, so overwhelming that she narrowed her eyes and turned from it. She envisioned the men where they had been, forming an image from the placement of the leader and the light on his hood. It gave off no odor, yet its effect was strong enough to blanket his scent entirely, while the others disappeared into their cloaks.

"Leave," she growled, her voice rumbling through the extended chamber of her throat.

"She has become a dwelling place of demons—"

She felt the skin pull away from her fingertips as she planted her hands to help her stand.

"—and a prison of every unclean spirit."

Rough bone grew outward, covering each finger in a thick shell-like material ending in a fine razor. Rain collected and dropped from the thick fur that lined the backs of her hands and both arms. Her claws scraped against the cobblestones as she pushed herself upward, hunching over as she stood to let the curve in her spine push her neck forward. Her breaths exited her muzzle in a low growl.

She looked down upon them now, still masked behind the shining symbol on their leader's hood. It formed the image of an upright triangle with an eye at the center—the Eye of Providence. The light emanated outward and up like a signal fire in a starless night.

She braced herself against the wet stones. The other three men were ghosts, left for her mind to guess from patterns, movement, and reason.

She ran.

Rainwater sprayed from her every bounding step. Her arms and legs sprang off the stones. The street was a blur of scents, yet she knew everything that surrounded her—everything except for the men hiding behind the light. The shine of it reached her even as she raced from it. It burned into the back of her head, stretching into the distance as she propelled herself forward, air and rain whipping past her as though she were an arm of a hurricane. The wet smacks of the men's footsteps were a stampede.

She turned into an opening she knew from routine, a small alley which led away from her home. No reason to give these men a path to her flat—to her husband and daughter—once she escaped. If she escaped. She sprinted toward the old brick-faced shop where the passage ended. The shop had been closed since before she could remember. She launched from her hind legs and into the air.

A gunshot silenced the rain.

She smelled the burning iron as it buried itself into her back. She roared with pain. The scent of her blood engulfed her, pouring from under her left shoulder blade. She slammed into the slope of the shop's roof. Her claws cut into several shingles, splintering and breaking them loose as she scrambled up the slick side. She felt the light from their leader's hood staring from the ground behind her. She grasped onto the crossbeam at the top of the roof.

Her feet slid against the slope. Smoke poured from the gun barrel as it raised toward her.

A second shot. A second roar.

With a crack, her left leg gave out as though the muscle had been severed from the bone under the knee. She smelled dust from the wound—the bone had cracked. She slammed against the angle of the roof again. Her claws dug into the wooden shingles on the opposite side of the crossbeam above her. She felt the water pouring down her face and chin and gritted teeth, through her fur and onto the skin of her back, rolling down her shoulders and stomach and legs. She felt the roof shake with impact beside her, again and again and again as each of the men landed, surrounding her as she struggled to pull her mass up the slope of the roof.

She sensed the punch coming before it landed. The blade extended from the man's arm and plunged into her back. She tried to pull herself up, but the muscle in her shoulder gave out. She tried to kick but pain ran up her leg. She hit the roof once more. A second blade, one held by another man flanking her, broke through her ribs. She smelled it as the tip splintered the wood beneath her.

She snarled and water flooded into her mouth. She breathed it in. She felt her body give out. She slid back on the roof, one claw still embedded over the other side of the peak. She heard the roof groan around her. Through the spotlight shining from their leader's head, she could sense traces of leather and glass as he stepped onto the crossbeam above. In his leather gloves was a glass vial.

He knelt down. She lifted her eyes to see him. He was a shadow beneath a stream of white fire.

"For the life of the flesh is in the blood," he said. "And I have given it for you on the altar to make atonement for your souls . . . "

The cloaks around her fluttered. She saw each of the other three men, their chests exposed as they spread their coverings out to hide her from the rain.

" . . . for it is the blood that makes atonement by the life."

CHAPTER 1

"*T*HE *SHINING* IS HIS BEST MOVIE. NOT HIS best performance, but still his best movie."

"That might be more of a Kubrick thing—"

Riley stopped walking. Nate took one more step before turning back toward her.

She stood perfectly still, arms hanging limp at her sides. "Come play with us, Danny," she said with an expressionless British accent.

Nate shivered in exaggerated horror.

"Forever, and ever, and ever."

"Creepy," he replied.

Riley put her hands out, turned her head, closed

her eyes, and let her mouth gape in a faux death pose. "Blood blood blood blood blood," she said, brushing the front of her coat with her gloved hand. "Everywhere blood." She laughed.

"It's especially creepy because you look like them," Nate deadpanned. "Except, you know, singular."

"Ouch." Riley contorted her face as though she'd been physically struck. She kicked one foot out to continue their walk from Nate's mom's truck to the bench in front of Riley's apartment building.

"I meant when they were alive," Nate offered, following.

"That doesn't make it better." She swept a hand over the wood before turning and dropping onto it. "Those were freaky-looking girls."

"I think that was the point," Nate said as he took his seat on the bench against the opposite armrest. "Wouldn't have been as tense if the girls didn't seem a bit off in the beginning."

"True," Riley said, nodding, perhaps only partially listening.

She leaned back to look up at the stars. Nate followed her gaze upward to the nearly full moon above their heads, and then back down to her. The moonlight made her skin an even brighter shade of pale. He remembered a joke he'd made the year before to a few friends about her being able to disappear if she ran into the snow naked, until he realized the joke probably made them picture her that way. His new joke was that between the pale skin, the black hair, and the dark eye shadow she typically wore, she was one black spot on her nose away from becoming a panda.

"You know," he said, pulling his mind away from his lame jokes, "there are some people who believe that *The Shining* was Kubrick's way of confessing that he helped fake the moon landing."

She cocked her head at him.

"Seriously," he replied, nodding. "There are people who actually believe this. They say he was recruited by NASA to fake the footage because *2001* was so good."

"Wow," Riley said, "just . . . " She shook her head as though trying to rid herself of an annoying ache. "Anyway, what about you?"

"Oh, the landing was totally fake," Nate replied with a cocky grin. "Totally."

Riley rolled her eyes until they landed on him. "I mean, which was your favorite of tonight's movies?"

"Hmmm . . . " he said, thinking about the selections for that night's theme: Iconic Jack Nicholson Films Older Than We Are. *The Shining, Chinatown, Easy Rider . . . "One Flew Over the Cuckoo's Nest,"* he said after a moment. "Definitely."

"Yeah," she said, nodding more in memory than agreement. Her eyes moved from the stars to the street light bouncing between the buildings of downtown Stumpvale, or what passed for it. "That one was really, really good. He was amazing in it."

"Swept the Oscars."

"Still," she said, "I kinda like creepy Jack better than cool Jack."

She suddenly straightened her posture. She went silent, staring at the building directly across the street from them. Nate furrowed his brow. She turned slowly toward him, eyes wide and face nearly corpse-like in hue. She raised one hand near her face, one finger extended.

"Redrum," she said in a squeaky voice. "Redrum." She said again, bending her finger in time to the word.

"I feel like that should have been really obvious," he said casually.

"I know, right?" she said, dropping the act. "You think it's gibberish—"

"Or a cocktail of rum and, like, tomato juice."

"Sure," she said, "and then you see it in the mirror and wonder why you didn't think of that before."

Nate shook his head. "Maybe we're just dumb."

Riley tilted her head in fake contemplation, and

the angle brought out the width of her squared chin. "Maybe." She nodded as though impressed by his conclusion. "Maybe."

She took a moment to smile before releasing a long breath and settling into the bench's seatback. Nate did the same, looking up at the sky again. Even with only a few lights on the road in front of Riley's building, there were still exponentially fewer stars in town than at his place outside of it. More black between those he could see, as though they were either farther from each other or he was closer to them.

"There's Highlander again," she said.

She crossed her arms and pointed with her chin.

On the corner across the street, in front of the Chase Bank, was a man in a long, black coat, its stains visible in the streetlight overhead. Nate couldn't remember when they decided to call him "Highlander." Aside from the white hair pulled into a ponytail, he didn't look anything like Sean Connery. The man didn't have a mustache or a fancy hat. His hair was even too thin, as slivers of scalp shined between the strands pulled back over the man's head. Maybe they meant Connery without the wig. But the name was especially strange since Christopher Lambert was the actual Highlander, and Connery was just his teacher who got his head cut off. Still, they'd always called him that, ever since they'd first started noticing him around the town years before.

"It's sad," Riley whispered.

The man bent to rummage through a trash can chained to the streetlight on the corner. The light reflected off the skin on his head like a halo from an old painting of a holy figure.

"Being homeless at that age," she continued.

"Sad to be homeless at any age."

She nodded absently.

The man emerged from the trash with a crumbled wrapper in his hand. He held it to the light before licking the inside. His hands were covered in slick, black gloves.

Riley looked away with a sigh. She pulled at the one blond streak dyed into her hair and held its end between her fingers like a paintbrush, frowning as she looked at it.

"I didn't really get *Easy Rider*," Nate said to end the silence.

Riley didn't reply.

"I mean, I guess it was supposed to show the cultural differences and prejudices of the nineteen thirties and all, but then it just kinda . . . ends. You know?"

She released the blond streak.

"Felt . . . incomplete."

"Happens like that sometimes," Riley said quietly.

"Hmmm?" Nate tilted his head to see more of her face.

She inhaled deeply. "My dad really liked that movie. He talked about it a lot. He said it was very real. Not just then but also, you know . . . like the way people treat each other, how not everyone gets closure. He'd also say something about how there are connections in the world that we never notice." She looked at her hands draped over her lap. "Or something like that. I can't really remember."

Highlander ambled to another trash can in front of the bank. He vanished into the shadow between the lights, only the edge of his coat catching the brightness.

"Sorry," Nate said.

Riley faced him, perking up. "For what?"

"For not getting the movie."

She shook her head. "Doesn't matter to me. I'm sure my dad would have like a hundred reasons why it's great." She shrugged. "I thought it was kinda okay."

"I thought Jack's part would've been bigger."

She scrunched her nose. "Me too."

"I thought about picking *Wolf* instead but remembered it being really cheesy."

Riley shrugged. "Never seen it."

"We should've watched *A Few Good Men*," he concluded.

She chuckled. "He loved that one too. He used that line all the time."

"I remember you mentioning that," he said with a nod, trying to be reassuring. "Maybe next time."

"Nope," she said, shaking her head. "Next time is"—she looked up, remembering—"Movies Meryl Streep Lost Oscars For." She lifted her eyebrows at him. "Or whatever it is."

"Maybe we can do a supplemental viewing. Movie Sunday on Friday."

"Hey," she said, putting her open palms out, "I didn't make the rules—oh, no, wait." She brought her hands together. "I *did*. So I intend to follow them."

"It's like how they do *Monday Night Football* on Thursday."

She waved her hands in dismissal.

"C'mon, rules are meant to be broken, as they say.

Whoever they are. One of them is probably Stanley Kubrick."

She shook her head as though fighting the urge to delve into his silliness. "Remy and I already have plans that night."

"Oh," Nate said, like he'd just run into a stop sign he hadn't seen. "Have fun then."

"We usually do."

"Yup," he said, looking at the building across from them, a small hair salon that looked like the woman who ran it lived in the back room. "The exciting adventures of Remy and Riley."

She rolled her eyes before looking at him.

"What?" he said. "It's your fault."

"We didn't choose our names."

"True, but you did—" He ended the thought there. Her relationship was her business. As long as she was happy, and as long as nothing bad was happening, nothing else mattered. She'd been hurt enough for one life. It wasn't his or anyone else's right to add to that. They'd promised.

She stared at him, arms tightly wrapped around herself as though challenging him to finish his thought. She lifted her chin in his direction.

"We should probably call it a night," he said.

"Yeah," she said, relenting. "Probably."

He rose from the bench first but waited to follow her toward the door of her apartment building and up the steps to the front entrance. The branches of shrubs hanging over the handrails tossed long, swaying shadows over the stairs, like ghostly hands reaching to grab them.

"Well," she said, turning to face him, "we finally get to cross Jack off the list."

"Ha! You said 'jack off.'"

"Oh God," she said, drooping her shoulders. "Boys."

He chuckled. "Anyway," he said, straightening his chin to tower over her, "thanks for coming to play with me."

"Forever, and ever, and ever," she said, reprising her British accent.

He shivered once more.

She put her arms out for their customary hug. Her hair smelled lightly of the same lilac shampoo she'd been using for years. He thought of the times before when he'd placed his chin on top of her head, emphasizing how much shorter she was. It always made her grumble, which always made him laugh. It'd been a while since he'd done that. It was probably never that funny.

"What were you frowning about before?" he asked as he leaned away after a couple of seconds.

She blinked at him blankly.

"Before, when you were looking at your hair and frowning. What was that?"

"Oh," she poked at where the blond streak ended just beyond her shoulder. "I need to dye it again already. Starting to fade."

He chuckled. "Girls," he said.

Nate stepped back to wait as Riley ascended the stairs. He also used to joke that even three steps up she was still barely taller than him. That was probably never funny either. She entered the code into the keypad next to the front door.

"You don't have to wait every time," she said as she completed the combination.

"Gotta make sure you get home safely."

"Dude," she said, gesturing to the brick entrance arching over her. "I *am* home."

"Not until you get through the door. Then no crazy people can get you."

She pulled the door open.

"Except those in your building."

"Seriously, you don't have to wait every time."

"I dunno," Nate said, tossing his head to point at where they'd last seen Highlander. "You have some sketchy characters around here."

"Sketchy, maybe, but not dangerous."

"America, man," he said. "Anyone can carry a concealed weapon."

She stared at him incredulously, bracing the door open with her elbow. "It's way too late for us to get started on that."

"Those guys in *Easy Rider* know all about that. Or not, because they're dead."

She grinned and rolled her eyes as she turned toward the door. "Good night, Nathaniel."

"Redrum," he replied, bending one finger toward her.

The door closed.

Nate couldn't tell if Riley had heard his parting quip, but he hoped she hadn't. It wasn't funny.

CHAPTER 2

NATE KNEW EVERY CURVE AND SLOPE OF THE road leading west from the town. After hundreds, perhaps thousands, of trips from his house—to school, the museum, Riley's place, Oak Street Cinema, the plaza, the hospital—he knew every spot where the road dipped and bumped, and the two places where tracks crossed on their paths to the opposite sides of the peninsula. He even knew the exact place—coming around the second left curve after the brick and plaster figures raising their hands on either side of a sign thanking those who visited "Historic Stumpvale, est. 1883"—where a

29

logging truck had lost control and slammed head-on into his father's car. "At least it was quick," people told him, as though speed made dying less horrible. When he thought about it, which he had conditioned himself to do as little as possible, it was likely the reason he still drove far slower than his friends thought reasonable, despite knowing everything about this road. Riley would joke that she could run to his house faster, or that whatever film they'd been planning to watch would already have a remake by the time they arrived at his house, but it was only about fifteen minutes away even with his slow driving.

His headlights illuminated the mailbox in front of his friend Craig's place, on the left side of the two-lane street. The houses became sparser, the forest denser, the stars more plentiful as he moved farther from the town. By the time he reached home, the only house he'd ever lived in, the "neighbors" were far enough away that he had to drive some distance to see anything other than trees and the occasional deer or caribou grazing on the grass, or, on very rare occasions, lying wounded on the side of the road.

It was more than six years ago when he'd heard the loud thump and crack while sitting with his mother in the living room. She'd gotten up to peek out of the window before opening the door. He looked behind her, seeing the back end of a sedan speeding down the road before noticing the animal on its side, pushing one hind leg helplessly against the asphalt. He heard its low, agonized moan from where he stood on the single step from the walkup to the front door. "Dammit," his mother said. She motioned toward him. "Go back inside," she said before ushering him in herself. She was taller than he was back then, but not by much. She walked through the front door and into the kitchen. Nate barely saw the hand towel and large knife as she walked outside again.

He waited a moment before rushing to pull the curtain back from the living room window. His mother walked directly toward where the deer continued to kick at nothing. He remembered seeing her circle around to its back, brush its side, stroke the top of its head until it stopped kicking, and then plunge the knife into its throat. She held it there for a moment, head bowed as though in reverence, before removing the blade. She wiped the towel along the knife as she walked back down the road. He rushed to the couch before she was able to see him at the window.

He heard her close the trash can's lid outside before she came up the walkway. He stared at the television as she again walked through the front door and looped into the kitchen. The water ran. He heard the floorboards creak as she moved from the kitchen tile to the living room carpet. She sat down on the other end of the couch—her side.

"It was suffering" was all she'd said.

As though speed made dying less horrible.

Now, he reminded himself not to think about that day, as he'd done many, many times when driving down this road or looking out his front window, or seeing the kitchen knife in the wooden block on the counter, or even the Swiss Army knife in the truck's glove compartment. That was the first time he'd actually seen something die.

Trees along the road swayed in the wind. The moon and stars doused them in white light, as though the snow had either stayed too late or come too early. How was it that Highlander had been able to survive so many winters without somewhere else to go? Of course, for all Nate or Riley knew, the guy could have a home right in the town. He could just be some crazy old man who liked the taste of crumbs and chocolate smudges from the inside of other people's discarded candy wrappers. Considering the many types of crazy people populating the world, that kind would probably be among the less dangerous. Nate couldn't remember ever seeing Highlander without that coat, even in the summer. It was still fine for April, but in July or August, it would be too warm for a full jacket. Of course, he only ever seemed to come out at night. His hair was always pulled back and he always had that coat. It was like he lived in it.

The same joke had been made about Riley a few times. That was never funny, either.

Their entire second-grade class had gathered in the cafeteria for a short assembly, where their teachers and Principal McGovern explained that Riley McKnight's father had passed away from a sudden brain aneurysm, a term which none of them knew at the time. As McGovern put it, there had been no warning and no way to prevent it. He asked that they all please be sensitive and make Riley feel welcomed when she returned—which she did the next week, practically swimming in an army jacket that smelled like old cigarettes and grease.

Students had greeted her with sad faces. Teachers offered to talk about anything she wanted, anything at all. She didn't seem interested in any of them. She'd just sit by herself in her seat during breaks or against the gym wall during lunch, until enough time passed that their classmates would make fun of her—of how the giant jacket smelled like an old man and stuck out like a bell from her sides, her little legs sticking out when she walked. Even in second grade, Nate had known those kids were jerks.

The first thing he could remember saying to her was, "At least it was quick."

The first thing he could remember her saying to him was, "Not for me."

By the time she had stopped wearing that jacket, the smell had either faded, or he'd become so accustomed to it that he didn't even notice.

The last time Riley had worn it was three months ago, during an event held by her mother and a few friends on the city council, to mark ten years since his death. A big banner inscribed with the words "REMEMBERING CLARENCE MCKNIGHT" stretched across the path leading from Cedar Street into the town's plaza. The banner framed the fountain in the center so that people entering from that side saw the main spout peeking over the top of the banner as the little jets of water danced around the interior of the fountain's rim. People brought food and drinks, signed a book at the reception table, and received little programs with pictures of the family together. There were speeches and songs and stories about the past, and even a couple of big prayers. Nate remembered Riley glancing over to him from next to her mother in front of the crowd with their bowed heads. She'd shrugged.

In a town of only about five thousand people, the two hundred or so who had attended was a pretty high percentage. There were plenty of people neither Nate nor Riley knew, yet every single person in attendance knew both of them. Strangers spoke about how much they respected Riley's father, how sad they'd been when he died, how much she reminded them of him. Riley nodded and said thanks, and when each of the strangers left, she looked over to Nate and asked, "Who was that?" Eventually her mother had made her put on the jacket and parade around in it. The jacket was formless on her now, sticking out against her hips and thighs but wide around the waist she'd carved over the intervening years of gymnastics. She didn't fit the image of the sad little girl everyone had been ordered to treat kindly.

"It's not like a jacket is *all* I remember of him," she'd said, "and it's not like I'll ever forget."

Remy hadn't been there that day. Nate hadn't actually met him until two weeks ago, when Remy and his mom dropped by after school to give Riley a ride to practice. He had barely spoken and had avoided eye contact. His brown hair looked like a bird's nest. He was also thin, almost unhealthily so, and a few inches shorter than Nate.

Nate had made a point of standing tall, angling his chin upward and thrusting his shoulders back in his best attempt at intimidation. He'd wanted Remy to know who he'd have to deal with if he hurt Riley. Not that Riley wasn't capable on her own, having probably the strongest legs of anyone he'd ever met, but still, it was the best he could do.

It was his Bud White impression, Russell Crowe in *L.A. Confidential*. Or at least that was what he'd been trying for, complete with his dusty blond hair, neatly trimmed, and his narrow face, which was younger, proportionally smaller—and, he hoped, lacked the big forehead and chin butt. Remy had even looked away as Riley gave Nate a hug before climbing into the SUV's backseat behind Remy's mom.

It was the only time Nate had ever seen Remy at the school. His family apparently lived even farther away from the town than Nate did, way out on a ranch that Remy's family had owned since the settler days. Back when Stumpvale was an ironic name for what the loggers expected would be left when they were done.

Nate pressed the accelerator lightly to speed up through the last right turn before the straightaway toward his house, just enough to stay steady at the speed limit of thirty-five. Not that anyone else actually followed that limit. He couldn't see it at night, but at the end of the turn was a dirt road that led a ways into the forest before trailing off into a narrow footpath that curved around trees and rocks. After walking for about forty-five minutes, you would arrive at a stream that crossed the trail of stomped dirt and grass. This was Patrick Wallace Creek, named in honor of his father. Or at least that's what his mother always told him during their annual pilgrimages deep inside the forest. Not that there was a sign or anything to prove that this random stretch of bubbling water was named anything, let alone after his father. He'd heard others mention it as well. Even if the city council hadn't officially named the area, Nate and his mom had, and for her that would be enough.

During each of their trips Nate would sit on top of a rock shaped like a camelback. He'd stare down at the water rippling against its side, splashing through where the rock jutted into the path of the stream before resuming its normal pace. It seemed like a temporary detour, a minor obstacle, before the flow carried on its destined path.

During every one of these pilgrimages to the creek on the anniversary of his father's death, Nate's mother would sit with her bare feet just at the edge of the water. The trips were never fun—an annoying walk in, a silent time sitting and staring at ceaselessly flowing water, and then an annoying walk back to the car. In later years, they'd stopped in town for a couple of donuts at the Sweet Spot about a block away from the theater. They'd stopped making the pilgrimage when he was thirteen, a year before Sweet Spot was replaced by Antonio's.

He remembered bringing Riley to the creek one year when they were maybe ten or eleven years old. He'd sat on top of the rock while his mother took up her position. Both of them stared at the creek bed through the rippled reflections of clouds and treetops. This was their custom.

"Let's make a promise," he heard from the patch

of dirt in front of him. He watched Riley peek over her shoulder to see if Nate's mother had heard her.

"Let's promise to never make each other feel bad."

He could still picture her there, with pitch-black shoulder-length hair and large, nearly black eyes that always seemed tired, even when they were little kids. She wore a dull yellow shirt and jeans cut off at the knees. Her skin looked nearly transparent in the sun and was coated with a thick layer of sunscreen, which her mother required she put on before leaving the house.

"Okay," he replied. He looked to his mother as well. She hadn't moved. "I promise."

"Good," Riley said, nodding up to his perch. "Me too."

They both knew the scene probably hadn't gone exactly that way, but it didn't matter. The two of them had referenced that moment with each other so often that it had become the Truth. Even if nothing like that had ever happened, they believed it had and that was enough.

He left the light off as he stepped into the living room. No need for sight when he'd spent all but six months of his life in the same place. He left the truck's key on the living room table for his mother to see when she turned on the morning news shows the next day. He walked between the table and couch toward the staircase at the back of the room. No light was visible from under his mother's door, but he could hear the television clearly, the buzz of electricity, the line-laugh, line-line-laugh rhythm of an old sitcom. Always so predictable.

The wall along the staircase up to the second floor was filled with pictures from before he was born. The first picture was of his parents' wedding: his dad with a full beard and slicked-back hair and his mom with an amused close-lipped smile that seemed more satisfied than happy. Next was a photo of the apartment they'd had in town before moving here, then the two of them camping in the nature preserve outside the city, then a photo of them posing with some other people—whom Nate had met when he was young but couldn't remember—his father in a black suit and tie after his appointment to the city council. Lastly, at the top of the stairs, was a picture of the three of them together. Dad had circles under his eyes and a thicker, grayer beard, while Mom was still plump from pregnancy, her swept-back features more rounded than usual. Nate was a chubby baby wearing a bib with chicks on it, propped in a high chair, his parents kneeling next to him in front of the kitchen counter of the old place. People always said Nate looked just like his dad, but it was hard to tell what was under all that hair.

Dad had died a month after that picture was taken.

Nate had learned to tolerate walking past the

pictures several times a day, being constantly reminded of the man he'd never met, yet who influenced his entire life. It seemed that for every older person he met, from teachers to doctors to friends' parents, he was Pat Wallace's kid. No matter where Nate went, he always remained in that shadow.

He turned from the stairs into the smaller living-room area of the second floor, and walked between the couch and the TV where he and Riley had been watching movies just an hour before. The smell of popcorn and melted Milk Duds lingered thinly in the air. The upper floor, with its small entertainment area, bedroom, and bathroom, was situated above one corner of the lower floor. His mother liked to refer to it as "Nate's apartment" even though it was totally open to anyone coming up the stairs. His bedroom didn't even have a door.

What it did have was a clear view of the picture at the end of the staircase. Seeing it reminded him that in this place he'd always be a child.

CHAPTER 3

IMAGES STREAKED THROUGH NATE'S VISION: A patch of dirt, a blob of tree moss, a string of branches with frozen leaves, all in a smoky haze as though blowing away in the wind.

His view rocked heavily, like he was riding a boat or jumping on every step. Rolling thunder filled his ears, a stampede approaching from somewhere. From everywhere. Then a low growl grew so loud that it seemed to shake the inside of his skull. Thunderous stomps and growled breaths synced into a primal percussion, a deep, impenetrable rumble as his head became the epicenter of an earthquake.

Hazy trails wafted through his sight, twisting their way toward clouds glowing at their centers as though what he sensed had burst outward and dissipated throughout its surroundings.

His charging stopped. The mix of snarls and motion stilled. He surveyed the area. The colors ranged from dull to bluish gray, spots of black, all of them streaming as though melting or smoking. He felt hot.

A spot of red appeared in the distance and glowed intensely at him, calling, pulling, mocking him to catch it. The tree branches sagged low from the dense snow packed along their lengths. The snow beneath him flowed in tiny waves, trickling down the slopes and sides of rocks and tree trunks. It was fresh, he could tell. Behind him his own tracks glowed in his mind: long green prints fading to blue and then gray farther back. The light snow dragged against his feet as he ran. His steps were not the high-stepping motion of walking through snow; they were low and leaning, savage. Two distinctly different sets of prints led up to him. One pair was larger than the other. He heard himself sniff the air twice. The red spot lit up within the forest ahead.

The thunder returned. The rocking, the blurred haze of motion around him, all faded away as that red light called, growing with every bounding step he took. A red so deep he could dive into it. He could plunge his body in and destroy it.

The source seemed to blink with his pulse. It moved, a streak of red leading from where it had been to where it was now, and hinting at where it would be. It grew larger in his sight, its shape changing as it moved, limbs branching from a cylindrical center. He twisted through its tracks, the red streaks waving through his vision like smoke, until he could feel the heat coming from it. Nothing but an intense, pulsing red.

He leapt forward. A high-pitched screech filled his ears. He swung vicious clawing strikes at the red blob beneath him. He growled and roared as he dug into the motionless form. The shape of thin legs and a slender neck appeared in his mind. He inhaled and exhaled in stunted patterns, quick and arrhythmic. His swings were heavy-shadowed blurs of red on deeper red, arcing through the air. He dug his hands into the warm, pulsing color. He destroyed it.

The glow faded in front of him.

Through the haze of melting snow he saw one deep, brown eye, big and round and shallow. The deer's neck barely connected to the rest of its body. Its side was torn and mashed into something more like a paste than flesh. It was the same one he'd seen his mother put down. He knew it was. It, too, smoked. It glowed and pulsed. It melted into the ground beneath it. But, for some reason, it didn't bleed.

His hands did.

Tiny spots emerged and spread over his fingers and palms. Red filled the lines and cracks, over-flowing until each hand flooded with thick, nearly black blood. It brightened to almost blinding. Its weight pulled at him as it cascaded from the sides of his palms and the gaps between his fingers like he was trying to hold fistfuls of water. The glow overpowered him with light. It pulled him in. It burned through his eyes and into his bones.

Everything burned.

Nate woke up with a pair of grunted breaths. He spun onto his back. He lifted his hands in front of his face, invisible in the dark of the room. He rubbed his palms together, patted his wrists one after the other, then his chest.

He took several long breaths to calm himself. This was the third time this month he'd had the same dream—the first was about two weeks ago, and then five nights before, after he got back from dropping Riley off following their Jack Nicholson marathon. It was the first time he'd found the source of the red spot. He'd always chased it but never caught it.

His room greeted him with a single red light shining in the darkness. His alarm clock. Waking up at 6:30 every morning was bad enough. Waking up at 3:15 was even worse.

The red light was strongest around the numbers themselves. It dissipated from there, cast a glow across the edge of the desk and part of the comforter over his bed. Rounded folds were colored as crimson waves. But that still didn't explain the dream, or why it would return.

"Chasing a deer," he said quietly, reminding himself. "Slashing it. Claws. Blood everywhere."

He sat up in his bed, pulling the comforter over his legs. He patted his chest again, feeling the broken and flaking letters of his old gym shirt, the one he'd worn for his first two years at Edgar High, before he and his PE classmates Dean and Seth got in trouble for removing the P and R from the Edgar High Spartans' logo.

He remembered his mother's words from years before when he'd woken up screaming one night. "Dreams are about the things least likely to happen," she'd said as she sat with him on the smaller bed he'd first had in this room. "Dreams are the subconscious processing the day." She'd then walked him through the different elements of the dream. It was nice, having her there to reassure him, enough that he didn't *remember* that night, exactly—he remembered his mother's story of that night.

The first time he could remember having any part of the running-through-the-forest dream was four years ago, when he was thirteen, a couple weeks away from finishing classes at Allan Middle School. Months later, all that came to him was blurred motion and the forest. After the fourth time he had the dream, he'd finally sat down at the computer in the study downstairs and searched through a pair of dream interpretation sites:

Forest: *To dream that you are in or walking*

through a forest signifies that you are in a transitional phase of your life. Alternatively, it means that you are being weighed down and want a return to a simpler time. To dream that you are lost in a forest means that you are searching for a better understanding of yourself.

Running: Running alone in a dream shows your determination and motivation in pursuing your goals. You will rise above those around you and find success in your actions. Alternatively, it may mean that you need to hurry in coming to a decision.

Red: The color red suggests raw energy, intense passion, aggression, power, impulsiveness, courage, and force. Red is the color of blood, referring to our primal energy and survival instincts. Red is also the color of danger, violence, shame, and sexual urges.

Snow: Snow in dreams symbolizes your

inhibitions and unexpressed emotions. Alternatively, snow may mean that you are feeling alone and neglected. If you are driving in the snow, it means you need to be extra cautious about how you approach your goals.

He'd assumed then that his subconscious had been processing his general fears of high school. He'd tried to make note of the things which happened the day before each reoccurrence, but he always forgot those.

"Deer, claws, blood," he said aloud, a reminder of what he'd have to look up after school that day.

As his eyes adjusted to the dark, he saw the old familiar walls of his room. The bare white paint appeared to him as a slightly lighter shade of black, framing the posters on the walls and the bookshelf next to the door. He imagined the room lit up, as it would be in an hour or two when the sun peeked through the window over his bed, as he had seen it do every day for years. The posters were of movies he could admit to his mother that he liked: *Princess Mononoke* (his mom was fine with cartoons—they're for kids, right?), *Let the Right One In* (in the original Swedish—he'd only told his mother that it was about a friendship between abused children), *Road to Perdition* (his mother was surprised Tom Hanks would play a hitman), *The Goonies* (his mother had bought him that one—he still loved it though) and *Fight Club* (that one took a little convincing). He wanted to order a cool *Boogie Nights* poster he'd found—a cartoon of Heather Graham taking a photo while roller-skating (*It's a cartoon,* he'd argue, *they're for kids*)—but he didn't want to explain that he'd watched the movie with Riley when they were both fourteen.

The bookcase took up most of the wall facing his bed. About a third of it was filled with the DVDs he'd collected before switching to digital. Another third was still filled with books his mother had placed when they'd first moved into the house. His father's thick books on northern European and Mediterranean history, photobooks of Alaskan landscapes and animals, a second copy of *The Little Prince* that his mother had given him one Christmas, after forgetting she had already gotten him a copy two Christmases before. Then there were various novels that his school had required him to read and he couldn't sell to the next class. The top shelf was entirely his: biographies of Scorsese, Kubrick, and Nolan, a book of famous movie mistakes, some old video game strategy guides, and his first PlayStation 2, which hadn't worked in about seven years and had already been old when he'd bought it.

The darkest shadows fell right next to the bookshelf, where the missing door opened to the entertainment area outside. Focusing, he could differentiate the off-white carpet, the brown railing, and the yellowish wall with the darkened pictures, which he could imagine in the same way he could imagine the movie posters around his room. Memorization, familiarity, assuming patterns and connections from what was known and logical. After all, the place had been exactly the same for as long as he could remember.

He took another long breath before settling into bed once again. He pulled the comforter up over his shoulders. Hopefully he'd be able to get a couple more hours of sleep before starting yet another frustrating week of high school.

"Deer, claws, blood," he said again, hoping to remember but not to see them again.

CHAPTER 4

RILEY BOUNDED UP TO **N**ATE'S SIDE AS HE PULLED open his locker. "So," she said, "I saw Highlander again yesterday. The guy, not the movie."

"Yeah?" Nate said as he pressed the books back in the locker.

"Yeah, when I arrived at practice, he was sitting at the bus stop on the corner."

"Did he do anything?" Nate yanked his jacket free from inside the locker. The weather wasn't too cold that day, but he still needed more than a T-shirt, especially while waiting for his mom outside.

"Nope, just sat there."

"Sounds suspicious," he said. He glanced over to see that Riley was scrunching her face at him.

"Anyway, I asked Shaunna about him and she said she didn't even notice."

Nate shuffled a few books to make room for others he'd need that night.

"And that got me thinking."

Nate inhaled to speak—

"I know, first time for everything, haha you're so funny, shut up."

Nate frowned as he stuffed the last book into his bag.

"What if Highlander isn't actually a homeless man, but . . . " She paused dramatically, waiting for Nate to zip the bag up before continuing. " . . . a figment of our collective imagination?"

He cocked his eyebrow at her.

"Think about it. Have you ever heard anyone else talk about him?"

Nate thought for a moment, but stayed silent.

"*I* haven't. It's like he's invisible to everyone except us."

"You know what?" he finally said. "Maybe you're right." He nodded gravely. "Maybe our brains have been infected by years of subliminal messages, and we're seeing things that aren't really there."

"Yes," Riley replied, scoping out the hallway with widened eyes. "In fact, maybe we're not actually in school at all. Maybe it's our brains making us see things that aren't really there."

Nate nodded in exaggerated thought. "But then," he offered, "maybe you aren't really here. Maybe *you're* a figment of *my* imagination."

Riley gasped in feigned shock before switching to an accusatory look.

Nate closed the locker as though he'd proven his point.

"How dare you, sir," she answered.

Nate fought back a smile.

"I assure you I am real. Maybe you are the one who is not real," she said, enunciating each word.

"That's exactly what a fake person would say."

She gasped once more. Her eyes wandered toward the hall behind him.

"I rest my—"

"Yo, Matt!" Riley yelled.

"Sup?" answered a voice from over his shoulder.

"See?" Riley said, tilting her head with her smile.

"Very well," he nodded, again trying to not break character. "So then maybe Highlander is real too."

Riley scrunched her face at him once more.

"I rest my case," he said. "*Ipso facto. Post hoc ergo propter hoc. Persona non grata. Per . . . capita . . . other things in Latin . . .* "

Riley's shoulders shook as she tried not to laugh.

"*In vino veritas,*" Nate added.

"What's up?" Nate heard from over his shoulder.

Matt came around to stand next to them. He

looked back and forth between them through big eyes set in a chubby face.

Riley snorted. She managed to cover her mouth before laughing.

"Nothing, man," Nate said. "Don't worry about it."

Matt rolled his eyes before shuffling toward the stairs. "Thanks for wastin' my time," he muttered.

Nate waited until Matt was gone and Riley had recovered before continuing. "Or, you know, applying Occam's Razor and going with the simplest solution, maybe he's just a homeless guy."

"That's so boring," she whined.

Nate ducked under the strap of his messenger bag. It wasn't always big enough to fit everything he needed for the night, but it was better than carrying a backpack as he had in middle school. He draped his jacket over the top of the bag. "Or maybe there's an even simpler explanation," he said, "like Highlander is actually an alien."

"Ohhhh."

Nate imagined Riley's eyes going big as she stepped past him in the hallway toward the second-floor stairs.

"Like a scout," she said, taking the first step down.

The school had been built like a cruel joke on the freshmen. Their lockers were all on the fourth floor, which meant they had to lug their books all the way up every morning, all the way back down in the afternoon, and anytime they wanted to change books during the day. Students called it "the climb."

"He's gauging our defenses," Nate said as he followed her down. "He's trying to determine the resources his army would need to overthrow humanity. Searching for Stanley Kubrick."

"Poor alien picked the wrong place then."

Nate gave a confused look to the back of Riley's head. "I don't think people here would put up much of a fight. Probably abandon the town instead."

"I mean America," she said, continuing down

the stairs, "because anyone can have a concealed weapon."

"That's what we have the Second Amendment for, right?" He followed her around the landing between the two halves of the staircase. "To hold off foreign invaders."

She jumped from the third step down. She landed easily on the floor, her bag taking longer to recover than she did.

"A well-regulated militia," he continued, recalling the Second Amendment, "being necessary for defending the planet against alien invasion." He stopped on the last step. "Something, something . . . everyone gets an assault rifle."

She stared up from the ground floor, head tilted away from him. "I think that last part was only in the first draft."

He stepped down. "Well, Thomas Jefferson is gonna feel really stupid once the flying saucers appear over Washington. He's gonna have to call

Will Smith or something. Or he would, if he hadn't been dead for, like, three hundred years."

Footsteps pounded loudly on the stairs behind them.

"Yes," Riley said, stopping to let him catch up, "but I like to think they'd be amused by the irony." She took a quick step forward to avoid another student rushing by. "Excuse you," she said to the hustling student.

"Who was that?" Nate asked, looking at the big backpack clumsily swaying away.

"Probably some frosh tired from the climb."

"Which you didn't have to deal with nearly as long as the rest of us," Nate replied.

"Oh yeah, and it only cost me a month on crutches and weeks of intense pain," Riley countered. She'd sprained her ankle during gymnastics practice and had all of her classes temporarily moved to the first floor, mostly because there was no elevator. The school board had been afraid her mother would sue.

"A worthy trade, I'm sure," Nate said as they kicked back into motion.

He saw Mrs. Wald and Mr. Clarkson, his freshman and sophomore history teachers, talking outside of Wald's room.

"Oh yeah, half a year of competition was totally worth sacrificing in order to not climb a few stairs."

Nate saw Mr. Clarkson turn away quickly. "See, your words say it was worth it, but your tone says it was not."

"You picked up on that, didja?"

He could see her peeking up at him in his periphery. "I'm very perceptive."

"Indeed," she said dryly.

"You've obviously recovered though. That's good."

Clarkson and Wald went silent again as he and Riley passed. Nate took a few more steps before turning back.

"Yup," Riley said, "you're perceptive and I'm invincible."

Wald turned away this time.

"Sure," Nate said, "let's go with that."

The freshman slammed into the middle of the school's three, wide entrance doors. He seemed to struggle for a moment in pushing back the heavy wooden door. Brick columns framed the three exits from the school, designed to keep out the cold and contain the heat during the long winter months. The door closed with an echoing slam after he pushed through.

Riley stepped in front of Nate as they approached. The door stopped her momentum for a moment before opening. Nate's eyes stung briefly as they adjusted to the sun reflecting off the clouds outside, the entire sky white in the midafternoon. He held his hand up to look over the parking lot.

"Crap."

"What's wrong?" Riley asked, stopping to look back at him.

He sighed loudly, reaching into his jeans pocket for his phone.

"She's not here again?"

He shook his head as he scanned through the list of numbers to find "Mom." He listened to the ring.

Riley craned her neck to see around the cars and deeper into the lot. It always amazed him how quickly the school cleared out after the bell. Apparently, the time it took for him to get to the second floor, open his locker, switch out his books, close the locker, and possibly meet up with Riley was enough time for everyone else to leave, especially on a Friday.

Riley looked between him and the lot anxiously.

The phone continued to ring.

"You can go ahead," he said, moving the phone from his face.

"You sure?"

"Yeah, go to practice."

"All right, sorry, dude. Hope she comes soon."

He rolled his eyes as the ringing continued.

Riley hopped off the curb in front of the school. "See ya next week," she said, throwing a quick wave as she hustled toward Beth's blue station wagon waiting to take Riley, Beth, Janey, and Shaunna to practice.

"Dammit," Nate muttered as he hung up and returned the phone to his pocket. He pulled the zipper up the front of his jacket. It was dark blue with a smoky design off to one side, which could have been random strokes but looked to Nate like a Japanese brush painting of a bird, maybe an eagle or falcon, perched on a tree branch. He preferred the image his mind painted to there being none, even if he was wrong. He braced one hand against the cold brick to pull the door open, dropped his bag to the floor, and slumped onto the bench just inside the front entrance.

"Hey," he sighed into the phone when it rang a couple of minutes later.

"I'm sorry, dear," his mother said in a tired voice, as though she'd just woken from sleeping all day.

He sighed again. "It's fine."

"When's the next bus?"

He looked at the clock placed above the front doors. "Doesn't matter," he said. "I'll take care of it."

"I'm really sorry," she said again, low and painfully, as if through gritted teeth. "It just came on today."

"It's okay."

"I'll leave some money out for pizza or something."

"All right," he said, "feel better."

Nate ended the call with yet another sigh, then checked the time on his phone. It was supposed to be twenty minutes—give or take ten to fifteen— until the next bus to his side of town. Nate brushed his jacket and sleeves down as he stood. He checked to see if the bag had pulled his jacket up at his hip, and braced himself before heading back into the cold outside. The door flew back farther from his shove than expected. His hands went into his jacket pockets as he moved away from the school entrance. The bus would drop him off at the last stop on the bus line, and he would have to walk for fifteen or twenty minutes before finally reaching home.

Nate stared at the road ahead. A fence divided the lot from the sidewalk, a pair of long gates pulled aside to let the cars in and out. A row of shrubs lined the fence as it bent around the school and separated campus from the neighboring houses. He'd only ever met one person who lived on this side of town, a guy who had known Nate's father. Nate could just make out a pair of kids standing at the arcade game inside the convenience store across the street. The sound of rushed footsteps caught his ear.

Nate put his head down as he continued on. He gripped one hand on the strap across his chest and quickened his pace.

The footsteps became louder, approaching from behind through the set of parking spaces on his left.

He kept his eyes low and angled back, seeing the painted white lines of the parking spaces rise and fall off the jagged surface of the asphalt. Tread marks and stains and a piece of pink bubble gum moved through his vision.

The footsteps were still there. Slower but closer.

Black lines in the asphalt tried to cover where previous lines had been, but the covering never seemed to work. It only made the previous lines stand out that much more. A snuffed-out cigarette and a crumpled half-page of notebook paper flashed by. And the footsteps were still there. Two pairs of them, still behind and in the next set of spaces, much quieter, as though trying not to be noticed. The effort only made them stand out that much more.

He turned around.

A man and a woman froze as though stunned. The woman looked to be in her late twenties. She was tall and slim, with dark brown skin and eyes, and pitch-black hair. Her high, symmetrical cheekbones, narrow, defined nose, and strong chin gave her the look of someone who would have walked into a detective's office in a 1950s noir. She would have been wearing a dress in that, probably a red one, instead of tight jeans and a tank top showing off a pair of well-toned arms.

The man sulked behind her like she was his bodyguard. He looked mid-to-late thirties, although it was hard to tell, with the beard that hung down to his collar and the long hair that reached past his shoulders. He had a straight nose, and eyes that were either squinted or very narrow. One of the man's hands continuously pulled at one leg of his oversized khakis while the fingers on his other hand twitched, shaking the bulging sides of a wrinkled, plaid button-up. His slouch made it impossible to tell how tall he was, but he was likely a bit taller than the woman, who seemed to be model height, only a couple of inches shorter than Nate. The man's eyes darted away while the woman's focused.

"Can I help you?" Nate asked with more venom than intended.

"You're . . . Patrick Wallace's son, right?" the woman asked. There was a slight shake to her voice.

He glanced between the two of them—her, almost unreasonably pretty, and him, disturbingly quiet.

"We're friends of his. Or—" Her head twitched away. "—we were."

The man scratched his chest, hard, nearly pulling open the gap between two buttons. Judging by his age, it was a stretch that he could have been old enough to have known Nate's father. But she couldn't have been more than six years old when Nate's father had died.

"We just wanted to . . . "

Nate felt his eyes narrow at them.

"We . . . ummm . . . " she sputtered.

Nate looked from them to the far end of the parking lot. Even with his bag, he could probably outrun the twitchy guy, who was wearing pants that could fall off his hips at any time. Of course, there could be anything under those clothes—a knife, a pistol, any damn weapon he wanted. This was America, right? The woman's tight clothes probably wouldn't let her be armed without giving it away, but the long and toned limbs meant she had a chance to catch him, even without his bag.

The woman's mouth moved but no sound seemed to come out until, "So, um, anyway, we were . . . w-we were just, uh . . . "

The sudden change was puzzling. This seemingly confident woman had forgotten how to speak.

"We were in the neighborhood and we'd . . . heard you went to school here, so we . . . " She glanced back at the man as though looking for help.

He pulled at one of his sleeves. "W-we wanted to see if—that you were all right."

Nate furrowed his brow at them.

"You and your mom," the woman muttered.

Nate scowled.

"With your dad being gone," she said, as though fading away, "and . . . everything . . . " Her pathetic manner didn't seem to fit with her appearance.

"That was seventeen years ago," Nate said. "We're fine."

The woman slumped as the man continued to tug at his sleeve.

"That's good," the woman said as though she were speaking to a mouse on the ground next to her feet. She crossed one arm over the other and withdrew as though deeply shamed. The man pulled at his shirt, his eyes still darting from Nate to the woman's back, then away again.

Nate shook his head as he resumed walking. There were no more footsteps behind him. He continued through the gate and turned to the bus stop between the school and the nearest house on the left. He stretched up to see as far into the lot as possible. The two strangers wandered slowly toward the other side of the school, their faces still averted from him like he was the Lost Ark. He pulled his phone out before sitting down.

We were right, he texted to Riley, aliens are coming.

CHAPTER 5

AFTER HALF AN HOUR OF OCCASIONALLY LOOK-ing around for the two weirdos at the bus stop, forty minutes on the bus for a ride that wouldn't have taken more than twenty in a car, even for him, and a twenty-minute walk from the end of the line, Nate let himself into the house. Crossing the kitchen and living room, he stopped at his mother's bedroom door.

"You okay?" he asked.

There was a groan of acknowledgment.

"All right," he said. "At least you're alive," he muttered as he stepped away. There was a smattering of laughter from the television in her room. His view traced across the paintings along the wall, to the door of the study in the corner under his room, to the bathroom next to it, then to the stairs and the picture of his parents on their wedding day. His father looked back at him, frozen forever in a moment of time Nate had never known.

"Not what I meant," he whispered, reconsidering his last statement. He continued toward the study.

Dusty photo albums took up the bottom row of the bookshelf to the right of the door. He'd flipped through them a few times before, years ago, as his mother pointed out the photos of his father holding him as a baby, when he'd worn a little yellow hat with red devil horns and a blue T-shirt with yellow lightning bolts on it. The other three rows of shelves were filled with thick history books, and other tomes so old that neither Nate nor his mother remembered what they were, their cracked and faded spines blurring their titles until they were impossible to read.

At one end of the very top row were stiff

newspapers from twenty years before, when a series of murders had occurred around the town. When Nate asked his mother why she or his father kept those papers, she'd replied, "History needs to be remembered." Apparently the killer was caught after a few months and four victims, but that day's paper wasn't included.

On top of the shelf were more pictures, framed this time: Nate's parents atop one of the nearby mountains with the valley behind them; the two of them along with several others in front of a stream in the woods with shovels and pickaxes in their hands; another of his father giving a speech in the main hall of the Natural History Museum before the blue whale's skeleton was suspended from the ceiling. Single moments stored away, while all that came before or after was slowly forgotten. As though those moments, the ones recorded in these images, were the only ones that mattered. The only pieces of history that needed remembering.

Nate sat in the antique chair and fired up the

sleek laptop placed on the dark rolltop desk. Other than himself, the machine was probably the newest thing in the room by at least twenty years. As the machine hummed to life, he looked over at the closed closet door and up to the large map framed on the wall between the desk and the closet. It was a hand-drawn image of Europe, jagged black lines on yellowed paper. His eyes immediately locked onto Transylvania, east of the Habsburg Monarchy and just above where the Ottoman Empire stretched downward until being cut off at the edge of the paper. He remembered laughing when he first learned Transylvania was a real place, especially after imagining it filled with people who looked like Tim Curry in drag.

Finding the information he wanted took less time than turning the computer on.

Deer: Deer are representations of spirituality and grace. They are edgy and frequently run at the first sign of danger which means you may be nervous or tense. Dreaming of a deer in its natural habitat symbolizes a pleasant new friendship.

The deer had been in its natural habitat, but then . . .

Capturing a deer in a dream signifies marriage, children, or receiving an inheritance. To kill a deer means that you may be surrounded by people you feel are enemies.

Well, technically he'd captured it first, and then killed it. So . . .

Claws: *Dreaming of claws signifies feelings of hostility or vulnerability. You feel a need to protect yourself and your surroundings. You may also need to be careful with your words or actions.*

Being surrounded by enemies would probably make most people feel vulnerable and in need of protection and caution with their words.

Then came the big one.

Blood: *Seeing blood in your dream symbolizes*

life, love, passion, and disappointment. It can also
represent sacrifice. To dream that you are bleeding
or losing blood indicates that you are—

Nate's phone buzzed in his pocket. It was a text from Riley.

I knew it!

Nate leaned back in the chair and started typing out a description of his encounter with the two strange people outside the school. He noticed Riley typing at the same time. He was trying to describe the woman and the man in the shortest, most accurate way he could, without resorting to weird, when her next message popped up.

At Remy's. I'll call tomorrow.

He held down the delete key. He replaced his long message with a simple Will do. Have fun. It would be better to tell her in person anyway.

Blood on Hands*: To dream that there is blood*
on your hands means that you are feeling guilt or
regret.

He closed his eyes and tried to put it all together.

Nervous and tense. A pleasant new friendship. A marriage, child, or inheritance. Surrounded by enemies.

Instability and uncertainty. A need to protect yourself and your surroundings. Be careful with actions and words.

Life, love, passion, disappointment from feeling unfulfilled and pursuing foolish, empty goals. Feeling guilt and regret.

He combined these elements with those he'd previously looked up: forest (transitional phase, weighed down, searching for a better understanding of yourself), running (determination in pursuing goals, finding success, hurrying to a decision), red (raw, primal energy, passion, aggression, danger, violence, shame), and snow (inhibitions, unexpressed emotions, feeling alone and neglected).

As he mulled the dream interpretations over, it began to make some sense. Transitioning from a determined course to an unknown one would cause nervousness and instability, make it seem like enemies were around and protection was needed, and cause feelings of disappointment or anger. There was also a heavy note of caution—one should be careful when moving into new places, or when surrounded by enemies.

But, did he have enemies? There were a few jerks at school, but no one he would categorize as an enemy. Maybe something less literal, like his own expectations and frustrations themselves, a feeling that he should protect himself from . . . himself. Or something like that.

He chuckled again, amazed at what the mind can do, the images and themes it creates, even when the rest of the body is turned off. He cleared his browser history before leaving.

After he shut down the computer and flipped off the light, he became aware again of the sitcom laughter spilling through the gap beneath his mother's door. Her condition was the reason she hadn't been able to keep a job for the last ten years or so. Luckily,

Nate's dad had a good life insurance policy, combined with a settlement from the shipping company for pushing their driver to work up to twenty hours a day, so he and his mother could move into a decent house, even if it was a bit too far from . . . everything.

His mother had never been clear on what exactly her health problem was. Chronic something-something-itis, he expected. He'd seen it come on before. Her joints would lock and her muscles spasm like an electric current was running through them. She'd squeeze her eyes shut, her head vibrating as sweat beaded her forehead, and she'd grit her teeth through the pain. She'd let out a low groan which seemed to reverberate as the spasm eventually ceased. Some took only seconds. Others lasted long enough that he once tried to help her up from the couch before she yelled at him to stop. She'd isolate herself immediately after the first symptoms and wouldn't come out until the spasms and sweat and overpowering fatigue finally passed, sometimes the next day, one time a full week later. At first, she would knock on her door and ask him to leave some food outside for her, like room service. These days she'd leave some money and maybe the car keys on the table so he could get out of the house while she dealt with her problems.

Nate reached the top of the staircase. He turned toward the empty doorframe. She wouldn't be able to hide behind anything up here, unless she didn't want to leave the bathroom.

On one occasion, about five years ago, Nate had waited to hear her door open during one of her spells and then crawled very slowly, as quietly as possible, toward the top of the staircase. He angled to see between the floor and the stairs, but could only see the floor directly beneath him. He took one step down, bent low enough that the rest of the bottom floor came into view. He thought he felt the wind as his mother raced from the kitchen back to her room. The door slammed shut so hard it shook the paintings on the wall. That was the last time he'd tried to sneak a peek.

When he first learned of the menstrual cycle in

health class, he'd thought, through his own discomfort, that it may have been that. But what he'd witnessed had been too intense. There was no way every woman in the world would be able to deal with his mother's condition and still function. It would mean that at some point every girl he knew, even Riley, would start convulsing and be incapacitated for several days. It would be impossible for anyone to function normally like that. Whatever the condition was, the practical effect was that he was on his own sometimes, and even stranded for several hours before finding a way home.

Nate tossed his bag onto his bed and dropped into the chair in front of his desk. He stared at the clock on the corner of the desk for a moment. Tomorrow was Saturday, but he'd probably still wake up at 6:30 in the morning, thanks to almost four years of high school conditioning. Of course, an alarm at 6:30 was still better than disturbing dreams at 3:15.

Nate kicked his feet up onto the bed next to him. He stared at his bag. His mind drifted back to the fidgety guy who barely spoke and the statuesque woman who crumbled right in front of him. It was possible they'd known his father. A lot of people did. He'd been on the city council long enough that most probably knew at least his name.

His mother said he'd also been a volunteer firefighter and was instrumental in the establishment of both the Natural History Museum downtown and the Stumpvale Nature Preserve in the forest to the north and west of the city. That's why the creek was named after him. "An honor," some old guy had told Nate several years ago.

Too bad Dad'll never see it, Nate wished he'd said that at the time.

He couldn't remember exactly when his mother first took him out there. He was maybe five or six years old. He did remember his mother screaming at him when he dipped his little red and brown canteen into the water. She ordered that he dump the water out and never drink from the stream. On the way back she explained that all the water in the valley, including the streams that ran around and through the city, had been contaminated by an oil train that had crashed near the Annex Lakes about ten years before he was born. Although the site had been cleaned up, the water still required treatment from the plants closer to Juneau before it was fit for human consumption. Other animals, like the caribou and deer that wandered nearby, weren't so protected.

Deer. He tried not to think of the burning red dot he'd seen earlier that morning. Red, the color of passion and violence, shame and desire. Blood was red. It meant sacrifice and guilt. He reached out to quickly snatch the bag on the bed next to him.

One chapter for history, two pages of trigonometry, forty pages for English, a chapter for bio, and for his elective rhetoric class he had to start preparing a speech arguing against the Olympic Games as an economic stimulus. All before Monday.

At least there was nothing for PE.

"Weekend," he said to himself. "Screw it." He

spun in the chair, over-rotating past the path to the door. He pushed off of the seat and walked out.

He switched on the TV outside of his room. A syndicated talk show appeared with six big chairs set across a stage with gaps between each pair. In the first two were an older man with a stern face that shined under the studio lights like a burn victim's and a woman with a completely blank expression. On the other end sat another man and woman, both wide enough that the chairs squeezed their bulk nearly to the couple's arms. In the middle were a younger pair, a man and a woman, holding hands. Two security guards were visible behind the outer chairs. The bottom of the screen read, "We are in love but our dads hate each other." Nate muted the TV before the host could say anything into the thin microphone, which looked like it belonged on a game show.

Riley hadn't seen Nate's last message. He scrolled through other names, looking for anyone who would be as solitary on a Friday night as he was. He settled on Craig, whom he'd sat next to in every history class since the second week of freshman year. They'd joke that the worst part of learning history was that there were no surprises. "It's not like there's gonna be a twist and suddenly, like, the Nazis win," Craig joked once.

"Which would obviously be terrible," Nate had added. That became their thing: twist endings.

Yo, Nate wrote in his message to Craig, what're you doing tonight?

The host said something that made the fat guy stick his meaty arm out at the audience. The reply came.

Chillin with Tony. Sup?

Nothing. Don't wanna do homework.

The older man on the other side jumped up from his seat. He gestured wildly toward the other side of the stage. One of the security guards started to step into the gap between the pair of seats.

Then why aren't you here by now?

OMW.

Nate turned off the television, threw the remote down, and rushed down the stairs.

"Hey Mom," he said, knocking on his mother's bedroom door, "you awake in there?"

He heard the television, the bed springs, and a low groan from within the room.

"Anything I can get for you?"

"No," she said in a voice so gravelly that it seemed to scrape along his inner ears. "You find the money on the table?"

He stepped away to see a twenty on the cutting board. "Got it," he said. "Mind if I use the truck?"

She groaned and shuffled across the carpet. He stepped back to look at the paintings along the wall outside her bedroom. They'd also been there as long as he could remember. One was a cityscape like those he imagined in old European towns, done in black, white, and gray, and almost entirely shadow with very few lines. The buildings were visible only by the light of lampposts and illuminated rooms which suggested their shape. White flakes of snow fell on the city like little gaps in the night. Another painting, on the far end of the wall, was an abstract of swirls and blurs which his mother had told him was meant to be a woman staring at the stars. Nate always saw it as a stream running past a pile of cinnamon rolls.

In the middle of the wall was his favorite, a landscape of craggy mountain plateaus in mostly red with some yellow, orange, and brown. It all looked like fire. Light, thin colors in the background and stray brushstrokes over the foreground created layers like a painted-over collage. This piece always stood out so sharply amid the muted tones of the others and the wall behind it.

He remembered telling his mother he liked it. She'd replied that it was painted by a distant relative on her mother's side. One of the first Tlingit artists to have his artwork displayed in a state art museum. Sadly the artist had been dead for years by that time. Still, at least some part of him lived on, his mother had said, through history or influence. People may not remember his name, but they would remember the work. That was almost as important.

He heard the shuffle of feet on the floor and then the key sliding through the gap beneath the door. "Thanks," he said, bending down to get it.

"Be careful," she said. He heard her moving back across the room. "Full moon out tonight."

"What was that?" he said, already moving away.

"Nothing," she muttered.

"Oh, yeah, full moon. Sure," he said. "Hope you feel better."

She groaned as he stepped away.

He looked over the house without knowing why. He turned off all the interior lights but flipped on the one over the porch outside. It'd be dark by the time he got back, and he could get the key in by feel alone, but it was an annoyance he could easily avoid. Maybe those two strangers from the parking lot would be right outside on his doorstep. If they knew his name and his school, then they probably knew where he lived. He'd be easy to find, especially if either of them had access to a computer. But would they have computers where they had come from? Nate shook the thought away. He opened the door and stepped out.

The moon was already visible in the bright sky, faded and behind a few wispy clouds like the layers of the painting he liked. He'd never been able to see anything in the moon, no faces, no patterns, just disconnected shadows.

He turned the corner of the garage, again imagining the two from the parking lot appearing. This time they seemed to pop out in front of him like the twins in *The Shining*.

Come play with us, Nathaniel.

Shudder, shudder. There was still a chance he'd see them again. Full moon and all. Those brought out the crazies.

CHAPTER 6

THERE WAS A RUMBLE IN NATE'S STOMACH.

"Dude, learn a new move already!"

"As long as it works I'm gonna use it."

Tony threw his hands up in protest as Craig threw his up in triumph.

"Hell yeah!" Craig hollered. "And still your defending champion!"

"'Cuz you use that same move over and over," Tony replied.

"Then learn to block it."

"It's not blockable!"

"Yeah it is!"

Two dozen colorful fighters reappeared on the character selection screen. Tony clutched his controller tightly as he focused on the characters that popped up from under the yellow player-two frame.

"Look," Craig said, controller on his lap, "I'm doing you a favor. I'm helping you learn."

Tony narrowed his eyes at the screen.

"Online players are gonna beat you so fast if you can't block." Craig picked up his controller from his lap. "Until then I'll have to kick your butt myself."

Tony's upper lip lifted into a snarl.

Nate felt as though he could smell the moisture in the basement of Craig's house. Half of the room was devoted to storage while the other half had been offered as a place for Craig and his friends to hang out. Craig claimed that his parents' logic was that kids needed somewhere to be reckless, and it may as well be in a safe place. Probably also helped that the basement was two floors removed from their bedroom so the yelling wouldn't disturb their sleep.

"All right," said Tony calmly, "how about we go one round without that hip-toss crap?"

"Whatever," Craig replied.

Nate's stomach rumbled again. A slight burn flared up in his chest. An empty pizza box from Antonio's sat on the table in front of Craig and Tony, who were on opposite ends of the couch. A few cans of soda framed the box. Nate looked down at the half-empty can in front of his armchair, which was angled slightly away from the couch. But he still had a good view of the large television mounted on the wall, with its array of wires cascading down like several thin waterfalls. Two unopened cans remained at the foot of the table. There it was again—that feeling. Better to keep that recklessness contained than unleash it on the rest of the world.

Nate groaned from a stabbing pain in his chest.

"You all right, man?" Craig said, hazarding a glance away from the screen.

Nate squeezed his eyes shut as his stomach seemed to rattle inside himself. The vibration rose into an aching heat in his lungs. It felt as though he would exhale exhaust.

"What the hell!" Tony yelled, skidding the controller along the table.

"Don't break my stuff," Craig replied.

"We said none of that hip-toss crap." Tony threw his hands up in protest once more. Through his shaking, Nate saw Tony as four arms, two heads, two pairs of eyes.

"I do what it takes to win."

The pizza box on the table was a jumbled blur. The smell of grease seemed to leak out in dense clouds.

"Yeah, right."

"Learn to counter."

Nate buckled as a feeling of hot daggers entered his chest. "No," he muttered. "No."

He gritted his teeth, feeling them grind together from the shaking. The scents of grease, moisture, and sweat filled his head. There was another scent as well, one he couldn't place other than it being that of an animal, or human. A scent that ran through Craig and Tony, in their blood.

"—all right?" Nate heard. Craig's voice.

The shaking settled enough for Nate to straighten up.

"I should go," he groaned.

"What's wrong?" Tony asked from his seat on the couch.

Nate used the chair to help him stand.

"You sure you should be driving?"

The character selection frame dinged a new choice.

"Fine," Nate muttered. "Should go."

"You need help or something?"

The shaking trailed off. A cooling sensation filled his body. He took a deep breath. The smells seemed to paint the image in his mind as he turned away: the pizza box and the soda cans, the couch, Craig turning to watch him, and Tony reaching for the player-one controller. The shapes appeared unclear but logic and memory made them solid.

"You sure?" he heard from behind him.

Another deep breath and the image disappeared. He righted himself, as though a weight had just been lifted. He shook his head. It always started this way for his mother too. Shakes and heat and then she was out. His heart thumped in panic. He heard a ding of character selection.

"All right." Craig said. "Take care of yourself."

Nate tossed back a weak wave as he stepped cautiously toward the stairs. Any twitch or imbalance could cause the shakes to begin again, the heat to stab through once more. Whooshing sounds of jumping and punching followed him up the stairs and to the basement door. Nate swallowed as he turned the knob.

"What the hell!" Craig yelled.

"I do what it takes to win!" Nate tried to move as little as possible while walking toward the front door of Craig's house. A brief burst of heat in his chest stunned him. He braced against the back of a dining room chair. Gray hues appeared over the table and the other chairs surrounding it, trailing into the kitchen ahead, toward the fridge and sink and microwave. The heat faded, and the gray of the room fell to black. He took a moment to gather himself before continuing on, cautious but hurried. The truck was at the curb outside, fifty feet away at most, then it was just a short drive home, which he could do as slowly as he wanted. He could even pull over if necessary.

The full moon hung so low and bright that Nate squinted as he stepped out. It glared at him like a spotlight. He yanked the door closed, twisted the knob to make sure it locked. The moonlight covered the entire neighborhood with a thin, white sheet, the pale tone of a hospital hallway at night. Silhouettes of the houses on the opposite side of the street cast long shadows which stretched to the curb ahead. They covered half of the truck in darkness, leaving a strip of light before its own shadow stretched over the blades of lawn grass.

A pain tinged his stomach as he moved down the

steps in front of the door. He sighed relief when no more came. Shadows grew from a tricycle, football, and other toys which Craig's little brother had left in the front yard. The washed-out color gave the yard an appearance like a lunar surface with the small toys as rocks casting shadows which other people saw as a face looking upon them. Nate kept his head down as he continued on, following the pathway toward the sidewalk.

A heat shot through both of his shoulders. He staggered as a lightning bolt coursed through his legs. The smell of wet grass rushed into his mind, the scents of oil and wood behind it. An image of the neighborhood pulsed in his vision, a spark ahead like sunlight reflecting off a piece of glass. It all disappeared as quickly as it had come on. He managed to remain upright.

"Are you okay, boy?" said a voice from within the opposing darkness.

He squinted to try to see the man through the moonlight and shadow.

"You seem to be troubled." The man's voice sounded like his mouth was filled with rocks. He started to come forward, a lighter shade of black over the silhouette behind him. Nate tried to focus on him. Over the man's head was a smooth cloth that ran down to his shoulders. And Nate had seen that old coat before, lit from above as it was now.

"Highlander?" Nate whispered.

The man took another step forward.

A fire exploded within Nate's chest. It shook through his bones. His whole body quaked. Spasms ran up and down each limb. A ball of light burst outward in front of him, replacing the man and the house across the road. Nate heard his breath leak from his throat. His skin burned and rippled from the inside out. He dropped to one knee. The light floated toward him, its center so densely concentrated that he could almost touch it. A thin mist wafted outward. "Isn't right," he managed to sputter as he collapsed shaking to the pathway. "Isn't . . . right."

"Truer words," said the smoking light. A form appeared within like the filament of a light bulb, brighter lines that emanated outward: one horizontal, the base of a triangle, with two others bent toward each other. It was so bright he felt it pressing against the inside of this skull. Heat surged from his chest to the tips of his fingers and toes.

The word "Help" leaked from Nate's mouth.

"I'm afraid there is none," replied the rumbling tone.

"Help," Nate said again as flames licked the back of his throat.

He writhed. Convulsed. His muscles seemed to move on their own as his brain was overwhelmed, wondering what was happening, why, and how to stop it.

"All I can offer," the voice continued, "is release."

"Help!" Nate screamed through the fire that laced the veins of his neck and along the nooks of each vertebrae and every other bone in his body.

"That's right," he heard from the light hovering several feet away. "Howl."

The concrete disappeared below him. There was only fire.

"S-s-s"—the word caught in Nate's throat—"s-some," he choked out, "someone!"

"Bring out the wolf," spoke the light.

"H-help me!"

The grass was smoke. The oil on the road, the asphalt, the metal and plastic of the truck, the wood and brick of the houses and the trees in the distances, all were vapor.

"A dwelling place of demons."

Nate roared.

"A prison of every unclean spirit."

Nate sensed a blur of action from above and behind. The shuffle of curtains echoed as though piped directly into his head.

"The hell is going on out there?"

The sounds pulsed through his mind as the images shook and melted.

"The hell are you do— Is that . . . Nate?"

A familiar presence entered Nate's perception. Craig's dad. Mr. Collins. They'd met several times before. He stared down from the bedroom window above, the smell of dried perspiration on his skin and fabric softener on the boxer shorts he wore to bed. Behind him the sweetness of clean sheets and the musk of an old mattress surrounded Mrs. Collins as she sat up to watch her husband at the window.

"Witness the abomination," said the man from under the hood.

Nate felt the fire within him begin to settle, lifting enough that he could feel the concrete beneath him. He raised his head, pushed himself onto one elbow.

"Show me what you really are," the voice said. The light appeared to pull inward in Nate's mind as though suddenly focusing, intense at the top of Highlander's head and spreading outward. It was a single high beam in the black night, its brightness dissipating into the dark. Nate heard footsteps from the floor above and behind him. They faded to nothing.

He placed one foot on the concrete, residual warmth and aftershocks still twitching the nerves of his legs and arms.

"Wha—" he said. "What's happening?" He felt moisture in his eyes as pain became fear and fear became sadness.

The light faded, replaced again by the silhouette of the hooded figured standing at the edge of the curb. The blanket of moonlight descended once more.

"Pray the keeper pities your ignorance."

Shadows waved as the man's coat opened. One of his arms disappeared into the dark.

"This world will not."

The arm came back out. Light gleamed off the length of metal in his hand. Highlander held the pistol up for Nate to see.

"Show me what you really are."

A surge ran through Nate's body, a chill which made him shiver. He straightened up and stood as still as possible. This couldn't be real.

"You carry the curse in you." Highlander lowered the gun to his side.

A joke. A dream. A figment of his imagination.

"There is no forgiveness for the cursed."

"Hey," Nate heard Craig's voice through the window slats in the door behind him. "What's going on?"

"He's got a gun," Nate replied, without taking his eyes off the weapon at the man's side.

Craig swore. "For real?"

A light came on in the house across the street. A figure appeared, peering from inside. Were hallucinations part of his mother's condition?

"Show them." Highlander rumbled.

Another light pulled Nate's attention to Craig's neighbors on his left.

"Show them your curse."

Nate's breath was slow and deep, trying to

remain as calm as possible even as his mind raced through dozens of questions. Was this the same condition which his mother had? Why was this happening to him now? Why hadn't it happened before? How can he stop it? Who is this man? Why was he at Craig's house? Why did he have a gun? There were no answers except one: don't get shot. His vision darted around, at people beginning to stare from other houses, the silhouetted hood ahead, the gun hanging from the man's side. Nate raised his hands cautiously. He hoped the pains wouldn't return. Not now.

"Look," he said, "I don't know what you're talking about or who you are. I just want to get home."

There was a sound like a single laugh. "We all just want to get home."

A shaft of light came on from above the door. Nate's shadow projected out and down. Highlander didn't flinch or react, as though he hadn't noticed the sudden pop of brightness. His low-hanging hood cast a shadow over his brow and eyes. Light illuminated the ridge of his long, straight nose, and the deep lines carved into his cheeks and jaw.

"Now you know who I am, boy," said the man.

Nate had joked, earlier, about whether he was homeless, a figment of his imagination, or the vanguard of an alien invasion. Any of those would have been better.

The stranger continued. "Let me see who you are."

There was a creek at the door. More lights from the houses around.

The man took several steps back onto the sidewalk. He put his hands out. Nate took the chance to back up as well.

"My friends," Highlander said loudly, gun pointing into the air, "I am not a threat to you."

Nate's foot hit the bottom step in front of Craig's house.

"You are good people," Highlander exclaimed loud enough that the people staring from the other houses must have heard him. He lowered his arms. "You are clean," he continued.

"Nate." It was Craig's dad again, from behind the door. "You all right?"

"I don't know."

"This boy," the old man proclaimed, the gun hung at his side once more, "he is not one of you. He is not clean. He carries the curse in his blood."

More lights, more people staring from the houses around.

"*He* is the threat." Highlander pointed with his empty hand. "He is the one whom you should fear." His voice descended. "A literal wolf in sheep's clothing."

"What's he talking about?" asked Craig's dad. He too could see Highlander. He was real. This was all really happening.

"Brothers and sisters!" The volume returned. Highlander spun around to see the surrounding houses. "Though you may not title yourselves as such, we remain allies in the struggle that is to come!"

His focus landed on Nate. His eyes remained in shadow.

"That between man and beast." His voice lowered. "The chosen and the damned."

Nate heard the door behind him swing open.

"Mister," said Craig's dad, "I don't care who the hell you think you are or what the hell you think you're doing, but you should leave now."

Highlander didn't move. Nate tried not to.

"Police are on the way."

Highlander scoffed.

"And if you don't leave right now"—there was the sound of a shotgun cocking—"there will be trouble."

Highlander raised his head. The shadow of his hood lifted just enough to see the dark skin sagging under his eyes. His lips moved silently, saying one word. Nate couldn't hear it, but the movement looked familiar.

It looked like he'd said "Sister."

A shadow dropped through the light above the door. Nate turned, looking behind him at the front porch, and saw a blur of fabric like Highlander's coat land right in front of Craig's dad. The coat billowed around the wearer. In one motion the figure wrenched the shotgun from Mr. Collins's grasp, broke the gun over a knee, and tossed it away. The figured shoved Mr. Collins back into the house.

Nate spun between the two of them, Highlander and this new threat. He felt a rumble in his stomach. The heat started to rise once more. His vision darted between the old man, standing straight-backed and tall on the sidewalk with the gun at his side, and the figure at the door, which seemed smaller, crouched down, a mass of cloth obscuring its form.

"We are here to wash away the sins of false gods."

Nate clutched his stomach as the shooting pains returned. The light burst in front of him, drowning out the shape of Highlander's long cloak. The grass yard, the houses, the people within them—images of them flooded into his mind, while the other figure, the crouched one, disappeared. Everything was clear from the road to the forest beyond. Everything except Highlander and the other.

Nate's confusion and fear and sadness merged into one thought: *get away.*

The voice bellowed from behind the light. "We are here to return the Almighty's blessing to this world."

Nate staggered back onto the grass, shuddering from the heat burning through him. The old man was a shock of white light, impossible to see beyond. The other figure, the "sister," was an empty void. She was nothing.

"We are here to make this world beautiful again."

Nate's foot hit the side of a football in the yard. He stumbled but didn't fall.

There was a spark of metal. A blade emerging from the empty space. From her.

"Run, boy," said the old man, turning toward Nate as he withdrew. The gun in his hand. The blade in hers. Nate glanced at the truck on the curb, the people standing in the doorways and behind the windows of the neighboring houses. He took a step toward the truck. Highlander shifted after him as though sliding across the sidewalk. He raised the pistol in his hand. "Run," he said again, gesturing Nate away from the truck. "There is no hunt without a chase."

As the pain faded, he ran past where the houses stopped, the streetlights ended, and the trees took over. He ran around one of the curves in the road which led back to his house. Did they know where he lived? They knew where he was. They had followed him to Craig's, to Riley's, all over. They must know where he lived as well. He kept running. He ran until his feet and legs burned from exertion and not from the fiery pains. This was different. Exhausted pain was better because he knew how it had started. It had started by fleeing from crazy people with weapons.

Nate slowed to catch his breath. A light breeze

shook the tops of the trees, which swayed as though each were moving to a different part of the same song. The moonlight stretched their long shadows across the road, projecting every needle as longer and thicker than they were. He knew this curve, he knew the entire road back. He knew that there was a bump in the road on the eastbound lane, which used to be a shallow pothole before it was repaired last year. He knew that the road straightened into another set of houses, one with a mailbox set into a metal statue of a buffalo. One more curve lead into the straightaway. One wide dirt path stretched from the road and deep into the forest. Trees lined the road all the way to the last house for a few miles. Home. The forest continued on until it reached Remy's place, but he wasn't sure if there were other turns or not. He hadn't been that way often enough to know it. He could only guess.

Nate felt the chilly air fill his lungs. He pulled at the sleeves of his thin blue jacket. Driving meant he wouldn't spend much time outside in the cold, so he hadn't thought he'd need to take anything heavier. The pains and heat had settled for now. He should use this time to get away. A light mist blew out with his breath. Police should be coming by now. Should be sirens echoing up the road. He listened for them. Friday night outside of a quiet town with little crime in the last twenty years. Officers would be available, but few were on duty and it would take a while to get from the station to the outskirts.

Nate patted the pocket of his jeans, pulled his phone out. Twenty-three minutes to one. How long had he been running?

He craned his neck toward the sky. Thousands of stars looked down on him, millions behind those. Dots in the sky, which people had imagined into patterns and shapes, constellations and directions for navigation. He'd never paid much attention to them other than to notice how vast it all was and how infinitely small it made him feel. He didn't see the connections between the stars, he saw the masses of space between each of them, between them and him. He listened for the si—

A fire ripped through his gut. He doubled over on the side of the road, braced his hands on his knees. He closed his eyes, groaning as the burn singed his ribs and into his neck and right into the middle of his forehead. Gray shapes wavered in front of him. The swaying trees became a clamor of creaking wood and blasting wind. A hundred thunderous sounds blared around him. A stampede. The dream came rushing back, the trees and snow like smoke, the pulsing red before him. The heat spread to his legs, muscles already burning from his run. Running. His hands gripped his knees, kept him standing, kept him from shaking too much. His hands were covered in blood from the deer torn open in front of him. He was burning. Everything burned.

Laughter drifted on the wind.

Another spike of pain dropped him to a knee. He clutched one arm across his stomach. Blood was lava in his veins, boiling and popping, heating the air in his lungs. A red tint appeared over the smoky, blue-green grays around him. Faint red spots glistened at the very edge of his mind. He struggled to stand, stumbled one step to the side, into the road. His knee buckled. He crashed hard.

A giggle. Light and airy. Free and happy.

His breath was static within his ears. His heart-beat was a bass drum echoing through a low cavern. The trees illuminated around him, still swaying in time to the rhythm of their own groans and pops. He saw every branch and needle, the moss growing on their trunks and the wet grass and dirt at their roots, the fresh growth in some, the rot of infection in others. He saw the path he'd taken from the Collins' house to here. It appeared as a trail wafting behind him, the houses in the distance with people wandering out to speak with each other. He saw the mass of burning light following him, a hundred feet away and gaining. It chased but didn't rush, slow and soft footsteps on the road. Then under it all was something else, something he felt his senses pull into under the cacophony blasting from everywhere, through the surge of quaking heat that scorched every inch of his body. Footsteps. Arrhythmic. Heavy-soft, heavy-soft, like a resting heartbeat. A hollow echo accompanied every heavy step.

Another laugh, like a little girl. It drifted up from behind him with no body to attach it to. It floated up from nothing. Then a click, and a flash of metal entered his thoughts. He seemed to sense a blade emerging from the void, moving around the road curving behind him. There was a whir as the blade disappeared again. A click to extend, a whir to retract. The blade came closer with every step. Heavy-soft, heavy-soft, click. Heavy-soft, heavy-soft, whir. And a little girl's laugh.

Nate pushed through the burn, trying to force his body to quit shaking, his mind following suit. Concerns and questions could come later, *now* was about making sure there was a *later*. He pressed his fingers into the rough surface of the asphalt. He couldn't feel the friction of his movement against the road, but he heard the sound of clothes being dragged along. He scratched at the road with his hands and feet, pushing with as much force as he had, anything to crawl even an inch.

"Sad pup," said the void behind him. The voice was young, almost singing with cheer.

Fumes of sweat and heat emerged as one cloth pulled back from the woman's face, another from her head. Her head appeared as a glowing red oval in Nate's mind, floating as if attached to nothing, as the cloak remained over the rest of her body. Red trails followed the movement as she turned to where the gleaming light drew closer.

"Stay," she said.

Highlander's light grew. The man's head was hidden, probably by the front of the hood pulled over his face, but the blur of light concentrated into a solid shape where the man's head would be—a triangle with an eye at the center. The Eye of Providence. Nate knew it from conspiracy theories about Illuminati symbols—they were in music videos, movie posters, Kubrick films, and on the back of the one dollar bill. He'd never seen anyone actually use it before. Light radiated out from the symbol like rays from the sun.

"All that was once yours," the low, rocky voice rumbled, "has been made ours."

The voice was fifty feet back and approaching faster than Nate could inch along the road. The burning in his body had dulled into a numbing throb that sent ripples through his muscles, and he groaned with each flash of pain.

"We don't fight fire with fire, as the saying goes," the old man grumbled as though to himself.

Nate's fingers scratched into the asphalt. The burning of his skin matched what he felt on the inside. His body gave out. He thought of his mother, the way she would shake, sweat, and become exhausted during her spells. Did it feel like fire coursed through her veins as well? Did she become tired from trying to fight it?

"We fight fire with the sun."

The breeze whistled as the trees settled into an easy swing. He saw a faint glow in high branches fifty feet from the road. Twigs and stiff grass molded into a little round nest where a small bird sat shivering atop three warm eggs. His own mother was still at home, alone. Her husband was gone, and their only son—the one person she had who still connected them together—was here, helplessly crawling on the road as two smoking figures descended upon him. Too helpless to even call her.

"For it isn't the heat you fear," the man continued. The light above him intensified, half blinding Nate's perception of the world. "It is the light."

"Please," he heard himself croak. "Don't."

"I am not the one you should pray to," said the light. "Sister Dove."

The burning head tilted toward him.

"Assist the little one on his journey."

Her steps were a staccato drum. She laughed—a stuttering, sickening melody rising to a sharp crescendo. Her face was a pulsing crimson mask in his mind, a streak trailing behind her as she stomped toward him, grabbed him, pulled him onto his back. She planted one knee on his abdomen.

"Young blood," she tittered.

"Please," he groaned once more.

He raised his shaking hand in front of him. Shaking from heat, from the sustained earthquake rattling through his body, from fear and regret and guilt. The hand burned before him.

Lightning shot from the woman's arm. He saw the tip of the blade drive forward.

At least it would be quick.

CHAPTER 7

THE BIGGEST SHOCK WAS SEEING THE BLADE sticking through the back of his hand. It didn't seem real. Its tip, shining at him in a way that was almost beautiful, hovered inches from his face. The scent hit him at the same time. Iron—in the blood, in the steel. He could move his fingers if he wanted. Most of them. The wound didn't even hurt. Until the first drop of blood slid off the back of his hand. It was real.

Nate screamed. The blade slid from his sight, scraping along nerves and bones. Red filled in behind it. The color of life and passion and violence dripped down the back of his hand, a solid line that seemed to spread outward into a thin mist like the filter over a camera lens. The rest of his body went numb, focusing instead on the metal that pierced through the center of his hand.

The giggling returned as Dove stepped back from him. A trace of moisture appeared within her burning face as she opened her mouth. She ran her tongue over the edge of the blade attached to her wrist. He heard her swallow. She breathed out deeply, as though receiving her first sip of cold water on a hot summer day.

"Without the shedding of blood," said the voice within the light behind her, "there is no forgiveness."

Nate stared at the hole in the back of his hand, and the shaking suddenly stopped. The solid trail in the center of the red cloud seemed to glow, like the stars had moved into his veins. The fire followed, beginning in one place and moving outward. His fingers twitched in front of him. Shocks of pain coursed through shattered bones under the skin. The tremor moved back up his arm, the fire again following. He felt as though he could see the blood in his veins bubbling to a boil. He could smell it there. It rushed into his senses, shining in his mind like sun reflecting off ripples. His teeth gnashed together so tight he could picture them pushing into the gums. His shoulder felt as though it would shake from its socket. His bones smashed into each other. He screamed again. The sound filled his head from both inside and out. Thousands of needles stuck through the inside of his skin. He felt himself ripping open.

Then the pain dulled. He burned. He shook. The world was a blur of thin colors behind the red glow that poured from his wound. But he felt it less, as though the nerves were deadening inside. The ground grew softer against his back and elbow. His arm seemed to detach, growing beyond where it had always been, the hand itself larger, pulling the edges of the wound with it. He heard a series of sharp rips and tears, dust from torn clothes popped up all around him.

The stench of blood grew so thick that he could taste it, spreading and coating the inside of his mouth. It poured from his teeth as they pushed from his gums and pressed together. The taste, the smell, surged into him, gasoline ignited by the fire coursing through him. His fear, guilt, regret, his concern for himself, his mother, all disappeared. There was only anger.

He dug his other hand into the road behind him. His nails scraped the asphalt. The skin pulled back from his lips and nose, scrunched between his eyes. He could feel the road, but it was as though a thick coat encased him, warmer than his jacket, which had shredded as his arm stretched from his shoulder. The arm's weight pulled at him now, seeming to extend out forever, heavier but stronger, before ending in a glowing sliver of drying blood. His throat quaked with a low, rumbling sound.

Nate pushed up until his feet rolled onto the

ground. They were longer, more balanced than before. There was a spring in his legs that he'd never noticed, like walking on the mats at Riley's gymnastics studio. He stared at Dove ahead of him, her head still floating, half-obscured by the blinding light several feet behind her. She was a burning skull. He lifted his hand in front of him. It appeared as a huge shape, dull yellow in color, ending in long, sharp points that pushed from the ends of his fingers. The wound was already disappearing. Some part of his mind whispered that he should be terrified. The rest of him screamed for blood. The blood of the light and the glowing skull. He wanted to dig his sharpened fingers into their flesh. He wanted to rip through their bones. He wanted to pull out their hearts.

A light laugh tickled the inside of his ears.

Dove was all fire and emptiness. The foggy light blanketed her, suggesting the form of her cloak. She took a step back, toward the light, one leg rotating out and around and behind the other. The second step landed with a hollow, metallic echo that vibrated from the foot upward. Nate sniffed at it instinctively. She remained a void. No scent escaped except for her uncovered face, burning into his mind.

"Here he comes," she said.

He drew in another sharp breath. Images flashed through his mind. He sensed the blood caught between the hairs on his hand, running through his veins, along the gritted teeth from his snarled lips, streaked down the length of Dove's blade. A drop remained at the side of her lips. Scents poured in from beyond, under those of the road and the trees and grass surrounding him. A pair of weasels lay in cold dirt spotted with rotting birch seeds. They were faint dots at the edge of his mind, but still he sensed them.

Nate growled as he pushed to stand. His back stretched up as though uncurling. He towered over the woman in front of him like she was a child. The heaviness in his limbs was balanced by a surge of strength he felt in every movement. He hunched forward, back still slightly curved, knees bent. It was more comfortable than standing straight up. There was no cold anymore. There was only heat. Only blood in the air. Blood and light, wafting in front of him, glistening red and blinding white. He growled again.

The veins in Dove's neck and forehead pulsed at an even tempo. Calm, relaxed, even as she burned into his vision. The rest of her remained invisible, except for the blood-lined metal extending from her arm. Her laugh was that of a playful child.

She looked back at the light behind her, a light which seemed to bore into Nate's mind. She turned back to him.

"Time to play," she said.

A roar shook through Nate from the inside out. He lunged forward. Massive clawed hands swung through the air in front of him. He moved without effort or thought. Everything was red. Everything was heat and anger and rage. He growled with each swing. Spit flew from his lips as he swiped after the scent trail, which followed the skull drifting back and sideways.

She remained out of reach. The metallic echo danced around him. He growled once again, frustrated. He should be able to catch her. Another miss. He should find the pattern and predict her movement. He couldn't. He snarled and snapped his jaws as she dodged away again.

He shook his head. It felt as though something were blocking him—blocking his ability to think straight, to apply what he knew and what he wanted. He wanted to stop. He wanted to take a moment to trace her movement, anticipate where she'd be. But his body moved without thought, as if the camera swung while he could do nothing but watch. He spun from side to side. Wild swings propelled him on. His toes dug into the road to keep him from toppling forward.

Dove vanished into another spiraling trail. Her laughter followed. He spun after her. His feet twisted under his weight, jagged asphalt digging into the tough skin. Sharp nails scraped against the road. His arm swung from behind his shoulder and around in a wide arc. He stretched to reach her, nearly falling as she remained just out of his range.

The blade pierced into his shoulder.

Nate roared as pain followed the blood streaking from the blade. He swiped his other arm to force her away. He smelled the wound in his shoulder, the sealing flesh of his hand. It didn't stop him. He spun toward where the scent of blood off her blade trailed behind her. She was swirls and spirals of scent in his vision—he had nothing to focus on. He swung wildly with every step. Highlander's light remained wherever he turned, always there, always burning into one spot in his perception. She disappeared into it and emerged from the other side.

Nate's breath was heavy. It poured out as a tempest in his ears. His shoulders rose and fell with every labored breath, each swing of his massive arms forcing him to exert more and more energy. He felt his legs beginning to loosen as he leaned back after another swing at nothing but air. He lunged forward again, another wild swing, another heavy breath. He hit nothing. He moved in circles after her. He chased an imagined tail. The faded trails of where she had been overlapped each other. All he could think of was digging his claws into her flesh. He wanted to grasp her little arm in his hands. He wanted to crush her bones in his fist and smell the blood spill from her veins. He wanted to rip that blade from her arm, the arm still attached. He wanted to plunge that blade down into the soft skin of her throat, so deep it broke through her collarbone and stabbed her heart. He pictured tearing into her chest cavity, breaking her ribs open and pulling the spine from between her lungs. Then he'd deal with the old man.

Her trail curled around him once more before it stopped. He saw the red of her face crouched in front of him. It burned into his mind. The blood coursing through her, the heat rising off, the sweat beading on her forehead and scalp, the intense light behind him—he saw it all in that moment. His arm swung back for one massive strike. He swung down. She shot up. Her trail flowed over his head. His body tugged awkwardly, trying to crane back as momentum carried him forward. He saw where her scent trailed up and over him. She landed on the road behind him. She spun. He sensed the blade carve up the back of his leg so deep that the iron scent of blood exploded.

Pain followed. Nate roared as he tried to strike at her. His leg shook and gave out beneath him. He crashed to the ground.

An eight-inch line ran down the back of his left leg. Jagged edges marked where the blade had caught on rough skin. Bits of cut hair floated through the misty blood that spread outward from the wound. He scratched at the ground. He tried to push himself up again. His weight forced him down once more.

Dove skipped in a wide circle around him, every

other step echoing on impact, as hollow as the playful laugh that followed her.

Nate felt himself trying to push up from the ground once again. He saw the gray of the trees around him, the moisture in the air, the traces of grease and burned rubber on the road. Blood continued to pour from the wound even as its ends had pulled closed, the skin repairing itself faster than he'd ever experienced. His hand and shoulder were already healed, but those were smaller cuts, not as long or as deep. He felt his heart pounding viciously in his chest, the stream of his heavy breath as it pushed past his jaw, slackened in exertion and desperation.

Dove came to a stop in the middle of the road. The glowing red of her face had faded into a darker hue. An odor of sweet oil over perspiration emerged as her cloak opened at the top. Lines of nothing showed threads tying the cloak closed at the neck. She reached into the cloak. A leather belt peeked out just below where the garment sealed the rest of her from his senses. There was the shuffle of fabric against thin glass. A sweet-scented cloth emerged from her side. She wiped the cloth along the edge of her blade, then stuffed it back into the void behind the cloak.

"Snack for later," she said in her childish voice, continuing her wide circle around him until she nearly disappeared in the blinding light several feet down the road. He saw the Eye of Providence looking at him from within the glow. It hadn't moved.

"Father," the girlish voice said. "Is it time?"

"Patience, Sister."

The light moved forward. The eye angled down to where Nate scraped his fingers on the road.

"There is a symmetry at play in this world." The craggy voice came over him like an avalanche. "A pity you will not be here long enough to appreciate it."

Nate dropped once again. There was no more fighting. There was no escape. He wanted to scream at the man, ask why he was doing this, what he was, how this had happened to him. His lips ticked and stretched. What came out were growls and snarls and grunts.

"It's almost a shame you had to find out this way. But more of a shame that you had to be this way."

His mother was probably still sleeping. Maybe she would notice he wasn't there in the morning.

"This was a beautiful world once," rumbled the voice nearby. "A beautiful, pure world. A gift to man from his Creator. All the beasts of nature were both his ward and his bounty."

Maybe his mother would learn about it on the news, through reports of a monster stabbed to death on the road leading away from the town. Or maybe it would be Craig's parents coming to the front door and asking if Nate had come home that night.

"This was a beautiful world of light."

"World of light," the girl's voice repeated behind him.

Would his mother know what had happened to him? That these people had come for him, and he had somehow transformed into this creature in an attempt to get away? Would these two, Dove and Highlander, go after her next? Was that why she always shut herself away?

"Don't worry, pup," the old man said as though sensing his thoughts. "Your death is not our goal. Not tonight."

Nate's eyes felt heavy as he remained prone on the ground. The wound on the back of his leg was almost closed. The blood was drying, matting the hair against his leg. The pain was nearly gone. He might be able to stand again. But then what? Dove had run circles around him before. Got him so confused that she could leap over him and slice through the back of his leg. He had no idea how to control himself. He'd only lose.

"Do you see, Sister?"

A low rumble came to Nate's mind. Not his own. Not a growl or roar. There were the scents of heat and metal and grease. An engine in the distance.

Something spinning rapidly with a slight whistle, moving very fast.

"None may stray from the path chosen for them."

The car screeched, still out of sight, as it entered the curve going toward the town. Nate smelled the burn of brakes and rubber on the road. A dim hue of light filtered through the trees, lighter gray among darker shadows. The smell and the sound were clear in his mind. Only a few seconds until the car would pass the trees blocking them from where he lay on the road. He'd be exposed.

"Follow that path," the old man said, "even if we have to be pushed."

There was another shuffle of cloth. Highlander pulled the pistol from his hip.

The car cleared the trees into the turn.

Highlander cocked back the hammer.

The car's brakes burned.

The gunshot shook the tiny bones in Nate's ear. The smell of burned powder and hot lead immediately filled the air.

The pop of the vehicle's tire was a small explosion. The brakes screamed as the vehicle—an SUV—veered wildly to one side before its weight carried it over. It flipped, crunching sharply against the asphalt. Metal pieces sprayed. Glass shattered. The vehicle rolled twice before skidding to a stop upside down, eighty feet away from where Nate remained collapsed on the road.

"For God has not destined us for wrath," the old man said, dropping the gun to his side, "but for obtaining salvation."

The smell of burned powder faded from the air, burned rubber filling in behind it. There was heat and broken metal, water, brake fluid, sweat, blood, oil, smoke. And, somewhere deep within the wreckage, a hint of lilac.

"None may stray."

CHAPTER 8

NATE JUMPED TO HIS FEET. **H**E GROANED FROM the sharp pain in his leg. Highlander remained still as Nate turned away, limping. Smoke lingered from the single shot. Nate took a few slow steps, gritting his teeth. He sniffed, focusing on the lilac scent in the air. He took off toward the car, pushing with both his arms and legs.

Dove remained still. She retracted the blade into her sleeve.

Nate staggered around the front of the over-turned wreck. Smoke and heat poured from where the metal smashed inward. All of the vehicle's weight had crashed against the road as it bounced and rolled.

Riley's hair hung down toward the car's roof like a waterfall splashing into a pool below. The seatbelt held her suspended within the SUV's tall cabin. She reeked of blood and something else that he couldn't quite place, a dry smell contained within the faint scent of detergent on her clothes.

Nate fumbled at the dull gray door for the handle. The long nails on his fingers—if they could still be called fingers—scratched at the lever. It didn't move. He wedged the claws in as much as he could, pulled and tugged for nothing, like a dog trying to turn a doorknob. He growled, then drew back and smashed one claw into the base of the door. He gripped his other hand over the top of the shattered window, and the remaining shards poked but didn't pierce his tough palm. He pulled.

The recently-closed wound on his shoulder pounded. Pain shot up the back of his leg. He felt the tension in every muscle in his body, all of them solid as he pulled at the metal door locked against the flipped vehicle. The stench of blood filled the cabin. It flowed from both of the occupants, Riley hanging from the passenger seat, Remy from the driver's. His face was a deep red mass, blood pouring in thick streams. Nate growled with the strain. Another scent came to him, strong and familiar.

Gasoline.

His muscles burned from tension. He feared they might give out before the door finally did. There was a metallic pop, a rip. He felt the door fail at the lock. He pulled the door back, seeing it break as he ducked into the car.

Riley's arms hung limp above her head. The dry scent wafted around her leg, indicating two cracks through the thigh bone. He sniffed around for more. Cuts dotted the right side of her face and along her arm. Hair matted from the blood.

Much more of the bone-dry scent came from Remy, hanging from the seat beyond hers. Blood dripped from his wiry, unkempt hair. Metal and plastic drove into his chest, locking him into position against the seat while air squeaked from a half-deflated airbag. His chest cracked inward. The scents of shattered bone and blood and something sour emanated from the long gashes along his face and neck. Riley's heartbeat was faint to Nate's senses. Remy's was silent.

Nate's lip twitched as he tried to speak. He tried to say her name. Instead, he voiced a guttural series of long, rolling rumbles and snorts. He shook his head in frustration before reaching for her, still upside down in the seat.

Nate cradled Riley's head as he reached across to pull at the seatbelt buckle. There was a pop and she dropped an inch before he caught her. His fingers pressed into the side of her face. His nails dug into her skin. New wounds opened up as thin slices in her cheek and above the eye. He opened his hand to hold her against his palm and not against the razors covering his fingers. He smelled her blood there as well, caught on the edges of three sharpened tips.

He knelt to pull her from the car, one hand bracing her neck while the other moved behind her hips, careful not to let the pointed claws touch her again. His own leg pounded with the effort of kneeling and stretching and pushing to counter her weight in his arms. She was lighter than he expected, almost tiny as he stood up from the wreck.

Her right arm dangled toward the ground. Trickles of blood rolled off her fingers. Her head slumped into the crook of his elbow. Half of her face was blood and hair. One hand and lower arm were dotted with small wounds and scratches. She must have brought it up during the crash, just as Nate had at the tip of Dove's blade.

He didn't even feel the wound on his hand anymore. Hardly felt the shoulder. The leg still ached but not enough that he couldn't use it.

Riley's left leg reeked of dust . . . cracked bone. She bled both inside and out. It soaked through her jeans.

Sister Dove's floating skull cocked as she

watched. Spots of dull red blood, his own, littered the road by her side. The light continued to shine behind her, the one big eye blocking the two under it.

"His plan," the craggy voice said, "can never be changed."

Nate felt the skin tighten between his eyes. His lips curled as he unleashed a low, rattling growl, more jagged than any sound the old man could make. Nate straightened up as much as he could. His back protested from the stretch. He hoisted Riley up until her entire body rested on one shoulder. Her head rustled the thick hair on his back. He didn't feel her make contact, he felt her push against the hair in the same way he'd felt the road when he first changed. He braced one palm on her back and crouched into a more comfortable position. Her bloodied arm drooped from his side.

His leg still throbbed dully. It was the left leg, same as Riley's. Dried blood remained on his palm and shoulder but the wounds were closed. The one on the leg was barely closed, but it could still open again, especially under strain. Riley's wounds were still fresh, still bleeding. He could smell the iron leaking slowly out, dripping and smearing onto the hair that covered his own skin. He shook his head as though trying to clear the scent. He focused on the smells in the distance, beyond the trees and the few houses of the neighborhood. He pictured the hospital, down the road, through the town and across the river. He smelled blood and gasoline. He had to get there fast.

Nate felt the strain in his left hamstring with every lunging step. It seemed like the rubber band of tendons connecting his muscles could snap at any moment. He could smell the blood leaking out of the newly reopened wound on the back of his leg. If he really focused on it, every bound tugging at the torn flesh, he would begin to feel woozy.

He focused instead on the scents of the trees whizzing by, the cold dirt between the trunks of high, swaying trees, and the road beyond it with thick layers of car oil and caked-on rubber. The wood and metal of houses and the buzz of electricity drew closer with every leap, which put more strain on the back of his leg. He pushed himself forward using both legs and one arm, the other bracing Riley against him. He dodged between the trees, visible as bluish-gray blurs. His breath was a hurricane in his ears, nearly covering the slight thump of her heartbeat. His body burned and ached, even beyond the wound in his leg. He didn't know how long he'd been running, how much longer he could endure this pace, or if Riley could endure at all. He focused on the road ahead. Nothing else mattered.

The trees came to an end. Houses lined the boundary between forest and town. A high, metal fence divided them. He groaned as he leapt into the air. He continued rising when he should have started arcing downward. The fence, just a little taller than he normally was, passed far below him. Finally, the ground on the other side rushed to meet him. He braced Riley between his shoulder and flattened hand, claws kept as far back as possible. He slammed hard, feeling the impact shoot through his feet and up his legs and into his back. It rattled his teeth. He groaned as he staggered forward. He could smell the occupants of the wooden house at the edge of the forest. The four of them were spread among three rooms. The slight scent of roasted chicken and potatoes lingered on them. On the other side of the walls were the heavy buzz of electric wires, the odors of other houses, other occupants, cold road, car exhaust, grease, concrete lined with grass and bushes. It all wafted around him in smoky, dulled hues mixing with the black of the night like an x-ray of the town. At the very edge of his perception, beyond and behind the spiraling trails of roads and buildings, was a wide field of grass and trees. The town's central plaza. The hospital would be south of there, along the water of the river bisecting the town. Above that, above it all, was nothing but black. No stars remained.

He took off once more.

Another time, he would have used what he'd known of the town to guide him. One landmark would lead to another, the gas station to the grocery store, the grocery store to the game shop, the game shop to the sandwich place—the haunts he'd been to hundreds of times serving as the link to the place he wanted to go. Now, guided by scent instead of sight, he didn't think in terms of streets and turns. He thought only of velocity. Everything else fell away under what he wanted to find. The wide field of the city park to the wet scent of the river to the stale disinfectant of the hospital.

Places he knew whipped by as he sped down the road, head and back straight like a missile seeking its target. Pain stabbed his leg with every push and pull. Fresh blood still poured through. Globs of spit flew from his mouth. Some of it floated over his shoulder, catching on the fur of his back or sticking to Riley.

She'd be disgusted if she knew. Her heartbeat was steady but faint. Blood trickled through her veins.

Nate pressed Riley firmly against his shoulder as he leaped over the newspaper box and trash can at the corner of the sidewalk. He growled as he landed, feeling the ache in his leg. He ignored the pain. Finally, at the farthest reach of his senses, came what he was looking for. Sterile walls and heavy chemicals shone toward him like a beacon. He dodged left as a beat-up station wagon turned into the intersection. He didn't care if the people inside saw him. The hospital gleamed ahead.

He raced down whatever open avenues he could, buildings flying past faster than he could process what or where they were, or whatever memories he had there. The plaza fell behind. He rounded the curve of the longer bridge across the river. His destination glowed on the other side. The light at the end of the tunnel.

Nate sprinted up the road leading to the emergency room. There was nothing but his own breath in his ears. Little activity elsewhere in the building. Ink and disinfectant stained the fingers of the few people in reception. Patients farther in were old and stale like rotting meat. He planted his feet, intending to stop and turn toward the wide door, but his right foot slipped from under him. His left leg strained. Right arm steadied himself against the ground. Left hand steadied Riley on his shoulder. He groaned in pain. A scream came from inside the door.

He straightened himself up before ducking through the automatic doors. A pair of receptionists were hidden under the desk in the front. Adrenaline flooded their veins. Hearts pounded like massive bass drums. One receptionist clutched a phone in his hands. A nurse hugged the wall of the hallway leading out of the waiting room. Her breaths were short, quick as a rabbit's.

Nate put his free hand out in front of him in a placating gesture, but they couldn't see it from their hiding spots. "Waiting room," one of the receptionists said into the plastic phone, "now." Their scents concentrated behind the wood, plastic, metal, and glass separating those who worked at the hospital from those who needed it. The nurse was a stiff blob just inside the double doors, blocking Nate from the help Riley required. He tried to speak.

"She needs help," he wanted to say.

What came out was a series of short growls.

"Help her!"

He heard a rumbling snarl. He snorted.

Nate roared in frustration. The others shook in their hiding spaces. They were masses of orange-yellow smoke to him.

There were footsteps down the hallway. Heavy and quick as someone ran, a small piece of metal stuck to his chest. A security badge.

Nate shook as he lowered to kneel his injured leg. He cradled Riley as he moved her off his shoulder, supporting her limp neck with his open palm and lowering her onto the waiting room floor. Blood continued to run from her leg, his too. Most of her face was a mass of dull red in his eyes, the three scratches looming as new blood. He carefully slid his huge hands out from under her and backed away, staying low. He moved toward the emergency room's entrance. He noticed that his back was to the door, in view of anyone coming in. Security passed the nurse pinned to the wall.

Nate sat on the floor. He bent forward until his stomach touched the ground. He rested hands and feet flat, arms and legs held close to his body, trying to make himself as small and peaceful as possible. He placed his chin outward on the floor. The security guard burst through the door, a mass of reddish orange with the scents of perspiration, adrenaline, and electricity.

Nate didn't move. He didn't make a sound.

The guard kept a buzzing plastic device out in front of him. He approached cautiously. Nate saw the security guard's scent lower as he bent down to check on Riley, a mass of blood smoking in Nate's vision.

"Get in here!" the guard yelled. "Get in here now!"

The guard rose again, Taser steady in front of him. Nate remained completely still. He lowered his eyelids and allowed his other senses to create the picture for him.

A nurse pushed through the door. "Oh God," she whispered.

The guard tapped the glass to the reception desk. "Get a stretcher in here now."

The receptionist rose from the floor to her chair, sat silent a moment before grabbing another phone. "Nurses to the emergency room. Nurses to the emergency room."

Nate heard Riley's heart make a barely audible thump . . . thump. Her blood smelled old and thick.

Stretcher wheels squeaked. Two pairs of heavy footsteps echoed down the hall.

Nate still didn't move.

The security guard took a few steps toward where he lay on the floor.

Doors vibrated on impact. Two more nurses pushed a stretcher. It creaked as it lowered. The nurses, one man and one woman, scooped Riley up. The stretcher creaked again as it raised.

The security guard kept his hand extended. His heart rate decreased as the stretcher squeaked back into the hall.

Nate still didn't move. He kept his eyelids low while looking up to the guard shakily staring at him. Nate sighed.

"Ummmm . . ." the guard said. "What the hell is that," he muttered to himself. "Ummm . . ." he said again.

The stretcher squeaked away. Riley's scent traced her path down the hall and into another room, one that smelled of cotton and gauze and antiseptics.

Nate felt the back of his leg tensing, pulsing, bleeding. He could smell his own blood dropping onto the tile beneath him, which was coated with a heavy chemical scent made to resemble what pine trees smell like to people who have never been in a forest. He felt comfortable in this oddly stretched position on the floor, as though it fit the contours of his bones—or as comfortable as he could be, given what had happened to him and Riley. And Remy.

He pictured the cut on his leg, down and across the back of his hamstring. A wound intended to injure rather than kill. Same as the ones in his hand and shoulder. None of them were fatal. Sister Dove had been playing with him the whole time. Highlander had told Nate to bring out the wolf. He'd known that Nate was . . . this . . . thing. This . . . monster. They had known exactly where he'd be. It had all been a plan. If accosting him outside Craig's house hadn't forced the monster out, then they would have stalked him, wounded him. If that hadn't worked, attacking Riley would have. Riley had seen Highlander too, outside of her house, at practice. They'd known about her. They'd known where she'd be. Probably knew her habits. They'd had a plan. They'd executed it.

The idea made Nate's head heavy. Or maybe it

was the blood loss. At least the wound could finally close, but at that moment, it still smelled fresh.

He tried to find Riley down the hospital hallway, but focusing took too much effort. It had been such a long night. His eyelids became heavy.

The security guard leaned closer to see him. He lowered his Taser to his side.

"Umm . . . " the guard said, leaning out toward where Nate remained on the floor. "Good boy . . . I guess."

Then Nate passed out.

CHAPTER 9

COLORS SWIRLED ALL AROUND. NOT THE BLOOD red or the shades of black, gray, and white that he'd seen before, but every hue he could imagine, oversaturated like those old movies with the color painted over the black and white film. Colors so thick Nate felt like he could bury his hands—or whatever his hands had become—in them. Large mitts and tough skin, fingers with four-inch-long razor-sharp nails that so easily scratched Riley's face. The nebulous swirls of rich color bumped into each other as they circled around him, enclosing him, pushing against his sides and through his vision as though trying to pull his attention away from the lone light ahead of him, which shined dully from a single point.

He moved forward, the world jostling as his long neck and heavy skull rose and fell with his steps. He felt the colors rubbing against him. He felt them nudging, then pushing, trying everything they could to force his focus away from what they didn't want him to find. But the colors only succeeded in making him focus more on the thin light they aimed to drown. It grew as he closed the distance. Shadows became clear to him. Not the smoky shapes of scent trails but solid overlaps, thick black over white. The object of his focus was like a hand-drawn sketch pasted in the center of a canvas on which an artist had dumped all his remaining paint. Something was waiting for him there. He knew it in the same way he'd known it in the dream he'd had before.

The colors faded from his peripheral vision. All that remained was this hand-drawn tree, fingerprints smudged in the shadows. Their own tiny swirls left in the center.

He didn't strike this time. That wasn't necessary. He reached out to touch the image, finding that his fingers had returned to normal. Normal, he thought, the word itself standing out as odd. The bones in the back of his hand were visible, and the skin at the joint of each finger made spirals. The tree opened inward as he pushed, hand flat against the door. He stepped into a room, stark and empty except for Riley sitting on the floor, an outline with her knees pulled up to her chest. Her skin was paper white. Face devoid of shadow, as though an intense light shined directly upon her. The blond streak in her hair was the only shock of color in this stark world. She looked up from the floor as he approached. Her eyes were marbles embedded in the flat canvas in front of him. Her face remained motionless as she spoke.

"None shall stray."

"What?" he heard himself say.

"A little push."

He saw her face as though the camera zoomed in. The strand of yellow brushed behind her left ear was the only difference between the two sides.

He felt a rumble in his throat. It was the same as when he had tried to speak at the hospital.

"You will not be here long enough to appreciate it," she said without moving her mouth.

Boulders rolled through his mouth.

Riley tilted her head at him. Her face was rounded at the edges, bringing depth to a flat place. Her skin took on a less abstract pallor, shadows extended downward from her brow.

" . . . are not happy," she said. Her lips moved but the voice wasn't hers, "but they've assured the matter will be taken care of for now."

Nate felt himself being pulled away.

"And the staff?" Riley said in response to herself. Shadows clung to her so tightly he couldn't see anything through them.

"We can't stop them from asking questions . . . "

Nate blinked.

" . . . but we can make sure their questions are never answered."

The ceiling tiles all had small punctures in the exact same places, as though they'd all been stacked up before a thin drill ran through them. He'd seen these types of tiles several times before.

"What do you mean?" he heard a voice say. His mother's voice.

"The council has promised that any evidence of the incident has been promptly and efficiently lost. As will any request for further inquiry."

"Good," his mother said.

"They're not happy," said a different voice.

"They never are."

Nate felt the muscles in his neck tense as he raised his head. He noticed no pain in his hand or shoulder, and not even a hint in the back of his leg. He tried to speak but all that came out was a grumbled sigh.

"Hey," his mother said, reaching out to pat his

hand as it lay on top of the thin hospital bed sheet. "There you are."

She smiled very slightly from where she sat on the foot of his bed. Her light brown hair was pulled back from her neck in a loose tail. A few strands of gray stood out in the harsh hospital light. Her oval face appeared unworried, but she seemed to strain to hold it up, like she'd gone almost the entire night without sleep but didn't care. The lights made mountains out of her gentle cheekbones, and crevices of the typically small cracks at the corners of her mouth.

He looked from her to the rest of the room, the television on the wall showing some news channel on mute, a table underneath it with a pair of shoes on top of some folded clothes, and a man staring at him from the other side of the bed. He wore a badge on his shirt pocket with the hospital logo of an H stylized to resemble an eagle in flight. A second man leaned on the wall behind the first. This one wore a police uniform. Nate tried to say something, but all he felt was a buzz in his throat.

The two men looked across the bed to his mother. She nodded. The doctor looked back as the officer kicked off the wall.

"Mrs. Wallace," the officer said, nodding to Nate's mother as he passed. She nodded back. The officer didn't see her nod as he opened the door to leave.

The doctor took a moment to look over the room. "You need anything?" he asked.

Nate's mother shook her head. The ends of her earrings jingled; three thin silver chains hanging from turquoise stones. Her hand remained over Nate's.

"I know . . . " The doctor paused. His eyes caught Nate's. "Well," the doctor said, pushing his glasses back up his nose. The doctor muttered as he stepped toward the door, "This should be interesting." Nate's mother watched as the door closed behind the two men.

She stood up from her seat. "Scoot over," she said, waving her hand at his legs. "Can you?"

Nate grumbled something. He growled sharply. It felt as though he'd forgotten how to speak. He planted his arms to push up from the bed. Everything except his voice seemed to be working fine. He moved to sit up, angled the pillow between himself and the wall behind. An empty IV stood next to him. The bed sagged as his mother sat.

"You seem to be recovering well," she said after a long breath. "Feel like you need to puke or anything?"

He shook his head.

"Must have been the exertion. Most don't get to cut loose on their first night like you did. At least not in the city."

She looked him in the eyes and tried to smile but didn't quite make it. He glared back at her. She looked away, breathed out.

Nate tried to speak once more. A low sound

sputtered out. He shook his head and smacked the bed with one hand.

"Hey," his mother said. "You'll learn with time. As they say, it gets easier."

He huffed heavily. He growled, a thin, nasally exhalation that was far from the deep, rumbling threat of the night before. His limbs looked thin and light under the bed sheet. There was a gap in the side of his hospital gown. He pulled it closed.

"So, where to begin," his mother said, looking up to the ceiling.

Nate scowled, shaking his head. He felt the skin bunch up on his face the way it had the night before, but without the fur or the heat. He spit out a few disjoined noises.

"It's muscle memory," his mother offered. "A sort of automatic neurological response to the change in form between human and . . . " She paused. She blinked toward him, his scowl greeting her, then looked away again. " . . . *Fenrei*." Another pause for breath. "Or *wolf*, to use the shorthand. It always takes a few turns to condition yourself to quickly recover."

Nate squeezed his eyes and shook his head. He huffed. He imagined the words he wanted to say, the motion required to say them: *What? Why? How?* They should be so easy.

"That's probably why you couldn't avoid the accident last night. You didn't have complete control of yourself."

His every breath was a soft growl.

"That is, if you choose to control it." Her voice went quieter as she spoke. "You don't have to." She had a distant expression, then it was gone. "I guess you weren't skipped after all," she offered, attempting the same tired smile. This time it succeeded in looking comforting, but he still fumed at it.

"Most parents only have to have one 'talk' with their kids." She added the air quotes before placing her hand flat on the bed again, elbow locked to hold her up. "Not our family." She shook her head as she stared at the wall of the room. "Your dad used to remind me about how we'd have to have the 'talk' with you someday. I'd joke about which one." She breathed out quickly. "We're not actually wolves," she continued. "I mean, wolves have tails." She attempted a chuckle. "But after centuries of mythology, it's easier to just use their word. Better werewolves than werebears or something even more ridiculous." She looked away and down. "I suppose." She closed her eyes for a moment.

Nate opened and shut his jaw. He exhaled a breath, added his voice to make a buzz.

"You're getting there," his mother said. "Anyway"—big inhale—"yeah, so"—long pause—"we're werewolves. Or lycanthropes, according to . . . others."

Nate shook his head in disbelief. She didn't see it.

"And I probably should have told you about that a long, long time ago, but when you reached adolescence without any signs of turning, and after everything that—" She stopped talking.

He slammed his hand against the bed to grab her

attention. She stood up to circle around the bed, sitting on the metal rail framing his feet. She couldn't look at him.

"This isn't something passed through biting, either," she said, "contrary to what the stories say. It's . . . genetic." His mother paused for a moment before continuing. "I'd hoped that we hadn't passed it on to you. It's rare but I have heard of it skipping a generation. I would have had to tell you eventually, but . . . " She paused yet again, brow furrowing as though about to cry. He banged one foot against the mattress. Her head drooped. "I'm sorry," she choked out, "I'm so, so sorry." She appeared to deflate in front of him.

Nate shut his eyes for a moment. He took his own deep breath, letting the frustration and anger flow out of him. Flashes of the night before entered his mind: the eye of light painted over Highlander's head, the laughter that followed him through the forest, the echoing footsteps, the stabbing pain through his hand and shoulder, the heat that coated his every bone until he and the entire world burned. The shot. The crash. The blood dripping. The lilac scent in the air.

"I guess talking about it made the possibility real." She turned her profile toward him, the solid, straight nose and firm chin, which everyone said he'd inherited from her. "It doesn't make any sense logically, but I hoped that maybe if I didn't mention it to you, then this would never happen." She sniffled, wiped at her eyes. "'Logically,'" she muttered. "Says the woman who spent years trying not to be a werewolf."

Nate felt his anger replaced by embarrassment, as though he'd forced her to confess a secret he'd never wished to know. He imagined the feeling of finally, successfully pulling her from her room during one of her flare-ups, only to then behold her covered in hair, with fangs and claws, shaking and whimpering and cursing herself for letting him see her like that. He'd exposed her deepest, darkest secret. He closed his eyes, took a breath, and braced himself. So many questions. They would come in time.

"Riley," he said at last.

His mother's gaze snapped toward him.

"She's okay," she said after a second to gather herself. "In the ICU but in stable condition." She turned on the railing to face him. "You did the right thing by bringing her here. Doctors said that, had she remained at the scene much longer, she would have been caught in the fire."

Nate's eyes went wide. "Fi—?" was all he could say.

"After the accident."

His brow furrowed. There had been the smell of heat and gas, but he hadn't detected any fire.

"R-Remy?"

His mother shook her head. He couldn't tell if that meant she didn't know who he was, or that there was nothing but bad news. Nate remembered Remy in the car, steering wheel shoved against his chest, organs bleeding through his mouth, drowning as he remained suspended in his car seat. At least it was quick . . . maybe.

"Me," Nate said. The sentence was so clear in his head, and yet he couldn't quite get it out. "B-because me."

His mother shook her head. "One-in-a-million chance you'd be there at the same time."

"No." Nate felt the word come easier. "Purp— Per—" He reset. "Plan," he said. "Planned."

His mother cocked her head in confusion.

He needed to choose his words carefully, use those he could speak. "Dove," he said. He made a fist and shook it. "Dove." He gestured, pulling one hand from behind the other wrist, like the blade which had wounded him the night before.

His mother's eyes went wide as she leaned closer. Her face went a shade lighter. "Sister Dove?"

Nate nodded.

Her mouth gaped. She straightened up.

"Old man," Nate said, easier this time, gesturing to indicate the light from Highlander's head.

"Virgil," his mother whispered. Nate saw the shadows in the corners of his mother's jaw as the muscles clenched. Her hand tightened into a fist. "Father Vigilius," she said from between her teeth. Her eyes narrowed. "They were there?" she asked.

Nate nodded. "Who are they?" he asked, finally feeling like he could control his sounds.

His mother rose from the railing. She breathed loudly as she walked to the door, turned, and crossed in front of his bed. He could see a snarl flashing at the corners of her nose, her fingers twitching as she walked. She paced back and forth. Her lips ticked and curled. "Virgil," she said again as a low rumble.

"Who are—"

She stopped with a spin. She stared at him. Her eyes had a red tint from crying, or from rage. Her nostrils flared. Her fingers continued to twitch. "They followed you?" she asked through gritted teeth.

He nodded.

Her stare shot away. "Is it . . . " She looked back across the room, shoulders rising with seething breaths. "No," she said, her fingers rubbing together as though trying to snap without finishing the motion. "They wouldn't." She paced back across the room. "What happened?" she asked, turning toward him.

"Craig's house," Nate said, feeling the control returning to the muscles of his mouth and tongue. "I felt sick. I left and they were waiting. Woke up the neighborhood. People watched. He told me to run. They chased me down the road. Dove," he put his hand out in front of him, "stabbed me."

His mother growled loudly.

"And then everything changed. I saw . . . smells. I was . . . " He saw the trails again, the blue-green-gray of the forest, the floating red skull in front of him, the blinding white pouring from the triangle looking up at him. His heart thumped against his ribs. "I was a monster."

"No," his mother said, waving her hand, "not a monster."

"They made me wait for Riley to show up."

"We're not mon—"

His lip trembled as he looked to his mother. She went silent.

"They could have killed me but they didn't. They made me wait there until she came. The old man said something about . . . paths . . . salvation." His mother tilted her brows in concern. The shot echoed through his mind. "And then he shot out Remy's tire."

He heard the screeching brakes.

"They swerved."

The metal crunch . . .

"The car rolled."

The shattered glass . . .

"There—"

The scent of blood . . .

"I ran over to pull her out—"

. . . So thick in his head he could taste it just under the salt that rolled down his cheeks.

"She was hanging there. So much blood. And they—the others—they just watched." His mother was blurry through the water in his eyes. "I . . . think I cut her. My fingers were . . . " He blinked out a tear. "It happened because of me. Because I'm—"

"No, no," his mother said, striding to the side of the bed once more, placing a hand on his. "It isn't your fault." She wrapped his fingers tightly. "What they did wasn't because of you. It was because . . . " She paused. Her eyes dropped away. "It's . . . what they do now, I guess." She shook her head, silver earrings jingling. "Wasn't supposed to be like this," she muttered.

"Who are they?" Nate asked.

His mother took a deep breath. She stared once more at the wall ahead. "The Order of the Hidden Blade," she said with a certain mockery. "An organization formed to keep us from causing harm to ourselves and others."

Nate scoffed at this.

"They must have known that you'd do anything to save Riley. That you'd run through the entire town to get her here." His mother paused as though in thought. He took a breath to speak before she resumed. "They must have wanted you to expose yourself to save her."

Nate stared down at himself in the bed. "I guess they did."

She squeezed his hand. "Hey," she said, leaning to look into his eyes. All the rage was gone. She was the same mother he'd always known. "That's not it at all. What they did was make you understand who you are. They made you see that this . . . condition . . . doesn't change you as a person. You're not a monster."

Nate shook his head. "I couldn't even see them. Felt like I wasn't in control."

"But you were." A smile ticked on his mother's

face. "You were in control enough to get Riley here to people who could help her."

"I hurt her," he said. He stared at his open hands, the fingers that curved into neatly trimmed nails. "Didn't—didn't want to."

His mother stood and stepped to the side of his bed. She pushed aside the empty IV stand and placed her hand on the back of his head. "You're not the reason she's hurt. You're the reason she's alive."

Nate looked away.

"You don't believe me," she said.

Nate shook his head.

She took a step away. "Can you walk?"

He looked at her.

She motioned toward the door. "She's waiting."

His mother left him alone to get dressed. It hadn't occurred to him that he'd arrived at the hospital completely naked, his clothes having been ripped off sometime during his change from human to . . . not human. It was a little embarrassing to think about himself passed out on the floor with his butt stuck out there for everyone to see. Of course, at the time, the headline would probably have been the werewolf thing, not the naked one.

He threw on the jeans his mom had brought for him, a dull green Henley—which he liked despite it having a large faded patch over the left side from when he accidentally washed it with bleach instead of fabric softener—and an old pair of gym shoes he'd forgotten he even owned. He pushed his sleeves up to his elbows, tossed the hospital gown on the table, and left.

He stepped out to see his mother speaking with the same doctor who had been in his room. The doctor spoke in a whisper. " . . . target her—" Their conversation stopped as Nate's feet tapped on the tile floor. The man had large-rimmed glasses, and his hair was high on his forehead and graying at the temples, giving him a long face and aged look.

"You did the right thing bringing her here," the doctor said immediately after seeing Nate step out. "You know that, right?"

"I know," Nate replied, adding a nod.

"Any longer at the scene and . . . well . . . " The doctor trailed off for a moment. "She's sleeping now, but you can sit with her for a while." He looked at Nate's mom, then motioned for him to follow. Nate's mom patted Nate's shoulder as she fell in step behind him.

"Her femur was broken in two places. Lacerations along her right arm and the right side of her face. The stitches should be out in a few days. The cast . . . " The doctor trailed off again as they approached a turn in the passage. Nate saw the three of them in a mirror at the corner of the wall.

"She'll have to undergo physical therapy for a while. Probably have to give up gymnastics." Nate wondered how the doctor knew about Riley's gymnastics, but he realized that Riley's mother had probably been there. She must have mentioned the team. "But she should be on her way to a full recovery. The other person . . . " The doctor sighed. "Well, at least Riley should recover."

Remy. Never did anything wrong. Wasn't even Nate's friend to begin with. Had Virgil and Dove planned for him to be there too? Had they thought Nate would turn to save him? Or was he just another victim? Collateral damage in their plan to make him expose himself as a werewolf in order to save the person who obviously meant more. Nate didn't know Remy, not really, but the guy still deserved better than to die for someone else's mistakes for no good reason.

Nate continued following the doctor as he pushed through a pair of doors with narrow windows. His mom followed, her rage from a few minutes before now completely forgotten. His as well.

"Don't wake her up," the doctor said, placing his hand on the door near a chart in a clear tray which was stuck at eye level. "Better she rest now." The doctor opened the door and motioned for Nate to enter. Whispers started just as the door closed.

Nate almost didn't recognize her there. Not because half of her face lay under several thick bandages, gauze wrapped around her head and across her nose and chin. But because she looked so lifeless. Stuck in her bed, clear tube poking into one arm, the other covered in several small bandages, and one leg in a plaster cast suspended in a sling from the ceiling. Even after her ankle injury years before, she'd been tucking her crutches under one arm and hopping down the hall at school within a couple of days. Here, in her hospital room alone, was a completely different state than Nate had ever seen her in before. A side he wasn't sure he could reconcile with everything else he had previously known.

The first tear fell as soon as his back hit the chair near her bedside. He saw the accident again: the screeching brakes, the tread of the tire popping and flying through the air in one large strip, the SUV jerking hard to the right, the vehicle flipping from its own weight. Its entire force, its weight and speed, must have come down on one corner of the hood and knocked the engine back, into the steering column, and into Remy's chest. His bones would've shattered immediately. Possibly even before the glass sprayed out in every direction like deflected rainwater. No amount of trying to shield herself would've helped. He couldn't tell when her leg had broken. It might have been during the first bounce, slamming off the console or against the edge of the seat. In the seconds it took for the entire vehicle to flip onto one corner, then bounce and roll twice, there was no telling what could have happened inside the cabin. Of course, the accident may not have happened exactly the way he remembered it. Over and over again as he stared at the bandages obscuring his best friend's face and wiped away the tears that covered his own.

He remembered their creek-side promise. Never make the other one feel bad. Whether it had happened that way or not, they'd adhered to that promise. They'd made it a part of themselves. Yet here she was, a little broken girl, because of him. No matter what anyone else said, it was his fault. If they weren't friends, or if he wasn't . . . whatever he was . . . she wouldn't be here.

She had been hurt, because of him.

"I'm sorry," he whispered through his tears.

Sister Dove and Highlander—Virgil, Father Vigilius, the alien invader, whatever the hell else he was—they had done this. They had made him hurt her. They'd brought pain to someone who'd already endured enough.

A red hue crept into his vision. His mother knew them. She recognized the name, well enough that it spurred her to anger. Wherever they were, whatever they were doing, he'd find a way to get to them. And then what? Be trapped again? Have his leg slashed and watch as they giggled and shined and destroyed anything they wanted?

That had been his first night. He hadn't even known what he was. But he could probably learn. There must have been a reason most werewolf stories were considered horror. He felt the heat rising in his chest. His hands began to shake. If he could learn to control these sensations, then he could use them as weapons. He could make them—Dove and Virgil—feel as helpless as they had made him feel. Hurt them as they had hurt her.

He could make them fear the wolf.

A few soft knocks echoed through the door behind him. Nate straightened. He wiped away his tears, along with the red spots in his vision. The door creaked open.

"Nate, hon," his mother said from the small gap between door and frame. "I'm sorry, but we should get going soon. Dr. Casey will keep us updated." He glanced over and could barely see his mother leaning into the room behind him. "She'll be fine. They'll make sure of it."

He looked back at Riley. She didn't move except to breathe. The blond streak in her hair really had started to fade. "Yeah," he said, "she will be."

"That's the spirit," his mother said as she leaned back out of the room, pulling the door open.

Nate walked right past his mom and into the hallway. She stepped quickly to catch up.

"Should leave here soon," she said, just loud enough to be heard over the sound of their footsteps bouncing off the walls, "or we may run into people who have questions we don't want to answer right now."

"You said I could control it," Nate said, moving straight on.

"Yes," she replied, "if that's what you want."

"How?"

She paused before answering. "It takes time." It didn't require any special senses to pick up the trepidation in her voice. "We need to talk to the Council first." Her footsteps were rushed to keep up. "Make sure there are no other . . . repercussions."

"Then let's do that," he said.

He strode toward the double doors leading out

of the intensive care unit. He didn't turn. He didn't slow. His path was clear.

CHAPTER 10

THE FLAG OUTSIDE THE SCHOOL HAD SPENT THE day at half-mast. While walking through the parking lot, Nate remembered the two people he'd seen after school on the day of the accident. It was almost impossible to believe that all those things had happened within the same twenty-four hours. The way they'd shifted, physically and verbally, after approaching him. He'd thought that maybe they were spies for Virgil, although until that night Highlander had always been alone when they had seen him. They'd said they knew his father. It wasn't until that morning that he even remembered encountering them—the dark, statuesque woman and the large, slovenly man. He'd have to remember to ask his mother about them when he had the chance.

The school observed a moment of silence during first period. Nate lowered his head as Principal Wilson read a poem about sailing with the wind to distant, unexplored shores. Nate kept his eyes closed. Under his eyelids he saw the SUV flipping, slamming onto its side, glass and metal flying from it, Riley upside down and dripping blood. He saw Virgil raise his pistol to shoot out the tire. He saw what no one else did. He opened his eyes again to a world that he couldn't believe was real.

He walked through the hall as though in a bubble. Friends asked him how Riley was. Their words were background noise. "She's doing well," he'd say, "recovering." They'd ask who the boy was, the one who died. He'd answer that it was Riley's boyfriend and that he didn't know him well, but he seemed nice. "Harmless" is what he wanted to say. He'd dribble out some story that Riley's mom had called him to deliver the news of the accident, so that no one would realize that he'd been in the hospital as well. Not like any of the students would actually call Riley's mom. Better to speak about someone than to them.

Craig and Tony popped into the room before Nate's biology class began. They leaned in as they spoke, as though conspiring with him. They pressed him about what had happened outside Craig's house.

Nate shrugged. "Crazy people," he offered. "Who knows? Police came. Said they'd take care of it." Nate shook his head, implied that maybe they had caused Riley's accident. He felt a slight burn in the center of his chest. He shrugged again. "Rather not think about it," he answered.

They apologized and asked if he'd visited Riley in the hospital. Nate told them the same story he'd told everyone else. He'd repeated it so often that he was starting to believe it. "This town was built on a lie," he remembered his mother telling him while coming back from the hospital, "a lie that people like you and I have to keep. If the others—the people who aren't like us—if they find out, there will be panic. You can't tell anyone about what happened. Not anyone. Especially not Riley."

Nate asked how Craig's dad was. Fine—bruised, but fine. Craig said it was obvious Nate was shaken, and they'd talk to him later. As they walked away, Nate heard the hollow echo of the heavy-soft steps on the road. The classroom door closed with a bang and a rattle like shattered glass.

He waited until most of the other students had cleared out before even going to his locker that afternoon. He changed his books in silence. He descended the stairs and walked through the halls alone. He barely noticed Mrs. Wald step from her classroom as he continued toward the door.

His mother had let him take the truck that morning. "Get back as soon as you can," she'd told him.

"Spend as little time in the open as possible, for now."

He kept walking, into the lot, unaware as he passed the point where the two strangers had addressed him, then got into the truck and drove. He heard the screech from his brakes as he pulled up to the stop sign in front of the school lot.

He slowed to a crawl on the first turn between Craig's house and his. Shining dots in the asphalt looked like glass slivers left from the accident. He thought he saw a couple of burn marks as well, but couldn't be sure. As well as he knew the road, he didn't know every little difference in color and texture. He sped up as another car approached from the opposite direction. He noticed a dent on its passenger-side front bumper, totally unlike that of Remy's SUV.

The road's curve ended in the straightaway toward other houses. He slowed once again as a small brown mound lying on the shoulder of the other lane came to his attention. A little deer kicked its feet against the road, inching slowly away until it slid from the road to the dirt under the metal barrier between street and forest. Nate looked away and continued driving. The deer must have caused the dent on the other car. His mind flashed to the deer he'd seen years before. It had been much bigger. His mother had wasted no time in grabbing a kitchen knife, walking to the animal, and doing what she felt needed to be done. It had been suffering.

Nate pulled over.

He opened the glove compartment and removed the knife before exiting the truck.

The deer was breathing heavily as it pushed itself under the metal barrier. Blood spotted the two legs he could see, motionless while those beneath it continued to struggle against the ground, trying to push away into the trees, as though the forest would somehow save it. The deer paused as Nate crouched down at the edge of the road. Its head seemed to shake as it stared at him. Its eyes were big and round and surprisingly deep. It was young and soft. Nate unfolded the knife.

He reached out to touch its head, as he'd seen his mother do. It stretched its neck as far as it could, kicking but failing to get away from him. Nate crouched next to the road. His bare hand hovered over the deer's head. His knife hand was inches from its throat.

The deer didn't look away from him. Its breaths were short and quick. It stopped kicking. Nate thought he could hear the little creature's heart thumping so fast it would burst. Its deep, brown eyes were large and wet, frozen in terror. Nate had always been told that the difference between humans and animals was humanity's knowledge of its own mortality. Humans were unique in understanding the concept and inevitability of death . . . But this one was aware. Aware and afraid. It shook as he brought the blade closer.

Nate felt the heat rising in his chest once again. He felt a tingle in his fingers, a twitch. He remembered the dream he'd had: the red-tinted forest he'd run through, the snow that burned around him, the deer's head nearly cut off by the blood-soaked claws—his blood-soaked claws.

He pulled his hands back. The deer watched him, still frozen, still shaking, as he stepped away.

The deer kicked against the ground again. It groaned with the effort. It scratched lines into the loose dirt. It rocked back and forth, trying to push itself into the grass on the side of the road. It lifted its head to look into the woods. It cried out a shrill noise, as though hoping something else would find it. Something other than the monster nearby. It was a sound of suffering.

Nate stood up. He exhaled what felt like a lungful of steam. He took a couple of steps back as he folded the knife closed. The deer's thin legs shuffled through the dirt, finding no traction. The sound followed Nate back to his car.

Another accident on the same road as so many others. The deer was lucky in a way—there was still a chance it could heal, however slowly. If the car that had hit it had been going faster, then it would have already been dead. The impact would have killed it. It also wouldn't have suffered the way it did now, lying broken on the side of the road.

"It was suffering," Nate heard his mother say in his memory. But did that mean he could decide whether its life was worth taking?

He placed the knife back into the glove compartment before starting up the engine to continue down the road.

CHAPTER 11

IT WASN'T THE PAIN THAT TROUBLED HER MOST, IT was the itching. An invisible hand had painted over her face, arm, and leg with a brush made of poison ivy. Her face was the easiest to avoid: the bandages reminded her that any scratching could open up the stitches and make the scars look even worse. Her arm was similar, with the bandages keeping her nails from her skin. The worst was her leg, where not only was the itch most intense, but scratching the most difficult. If nothing else, gymnastics had made her flexible. Even in bed, with the leg elevated, she could reach her foot with either hand. It was the thick cast that was the problem. Pain had a button—it was the first thing the nurse had told her when she finally awoke two nights before. Press the button to administer a small amount of morphine. It was never enough to harm her, just enough to take the pain away. The itching, well, nothing they could do to help that.

At least there was cable TV in her room, even if it did force Tom Cruise to call Jack Nicholson a "son of a gun." But that would come later, after the famous scene that her dad would quote every time he didn't want to answer one of her questions.

"Dad, can you help me with this?"

"Sure," he'd say, circling around to squat on the other side of the table in the living room where she'd do her homework.

"What's seven times nine?"

She'd look across the table at him, her eyes big with all the sweetness she imagined having at that time.

"I'll answer the question," he'd say. "You want answers?"

He had a sprinkling of gray in his pitch-black hair and a fading scar at the right side of his chin that he said was from running into a fence when he was a kid.

She'd nod. "Yes."

Sometimes he'd shout, sometimes he'd speak dryly. Occasionally, he would begin with "Well, as you know," or punctuate with a "sweetie," or a gentle chuckle. But his response always included, "You can't handle the truth."

After the sixth time, she'd come to expect this response. She'd still ask him for help, hoping this time it would be different. Then she'd roll her eyes and feel stupid when it wasn't. She couldn't stop asking him for help, and he wouldn't give it. After a while she'd ask just to hear the silly joy he took in providing the same answer every time.

"If I tell you the answer," he'd add, "then you'll never learn."

She pressed the button. She wanted the pain to go away.

🐾

They'd left Remy's house later than usual that night.

They had to rush to get her home, or her mom would throw a fit over Riley being out past one in the morning again. She knew their "dates" were silly—hiking in the woods around his house, playing card games with his little sisters, even building stuff out of his old box of Lego bricks, at first following the pictures and later making it up as they went along—but they were fun. Like she was free to be a kid again without worrying about being judged or being tough enough. The girl with the strong legs, the Army jacket, and the dead father whom it seemed everyone else had known better than she ever would.

Remy's house was an oasis, a throwback to what she imagined homesteads were like in the 1950s.

A harmless Quaker family living out in the wilderness. Parents raising their son so respectful and shy that she actually felt like a predator for pulling his shirt off once. She learned it was better to enjoy the company, enjoy the escape, and smile as they listed blessings before dinner, just as she did when her father would do the same.

The first time he ever took his hand off the wheel while driving was when it was wrenched away from him. Riley had barely glimpsed the end of the curve through the woods—and some kind of animal that had strayed onto the road—before the pop.

The seatbelt pressed against her so hard she thought it would break her collarbone. Gravity shifted. The world started to spin end over end. It was . . . unnatural . . . baffling in the moment. Her leg slammed into . . . something . . . she couldn't tell what. The metal crunching was a constant, like a bassline, the shattering glass a series of sharp accents. The shards were falling snow. She didn't even think to cover herself until the stinging edges slit her face.

There was a deafening, airy pop. She opened one eye to see Remy's neck swing back and forth, and his arms flail weightlessly. The rest of him didn't move. Gravity shifted once more, pulling her down against the tug of the seatbelt.

Remy's face was melting. She was stuck, held in the air, metal crushed in on her. She was a mouse trapped in a giant's hand. All she could see was her hair swaying downward, and the fabric of the SUV's ceiling sparking with slivers of glass as blood dropped upon it.

"This can't be real," she thought as the ceiling twisted above her. "Nothing like this can happen." She felt herself twisting against the chair. "Not to me."

Outside was black. Below were her legs, only now swelling with pain. Above was hair and streams of bright red pouring out like she was staring at her feet while standing in a downpour. Except that her feet were above her. "Not me," she remembered thinking, "Not—"

Then she'd woken up.

It was as though she'd dreamt the entire thing, until she tried to open her other eye and found it covered with a white pad that she couldn't shake off and didn't have the strength to reach for.

A nurse told her that she was lucky. Someone had saved her after the accident. It was a miracle. Her mom said the same thing before continuing in a whispered tone, "But Remy . . . "

She pressed the button again.

The throb in her thigh stopped. The pain did not.

"Ms. McKnight," said a soft voice through the door. "Are you awake?"

Riley looked around. A small tray with a sandwich and a bowl of Jell-O sat on the table attached to the bed's handrail. Must be sometime in the afternoon. Too early to act like a "son of a gun."

"I'm here," she said.

The door creaked open. "Umm," the nurse started as she peeked through the gap, "your uncle is here to see you."

"My uncle?"

"I can tell him to come back another time."

"It's . . . fine," Riley replied, remembering how several men at the memorial had referred to themselves as being "like brothers" to her father.

Riley heard talking outside as she searched for the remote. She pressed the mute button just as the door closed.

"McKnight." The man's voice was like broken pavement. "Do you know what that means?"

She shook as she recognized the man she and Nate had called Highlander, standing inside the door of her hospital room. His wrinkles made his face as craggy as his voice.

"It means 'son of knight,'" he said. His head made a slow arc of the room.

"What—" she stuttered. "What are you doing—"

"For you, this would be half true."

She tried to inch away but her suspended leg wouldn't let her. She angled her head, trying to look through the curtains over the hallway window, but saw no shadow of her nurse out front. Riley placed one hand on the rim of the tray, ready to swing it if necessary.

"You don't remember," the old man said as he reached to pull the chair from next to her bed. "I brought you here." He looked down as he sat, exposing the thinning hair scattered across his scalp. "I pulled you from the greatest wreck of your life."

His face was clean-shaven, without a hint of the dirt or grease she assumed he'd have. He wore a collared shirt with the top button open to show strands of a gold necklace underneath. He didn't have any gloves or coat, just a leather bag he placed across his lap.

"I'm sorry about the boy," he said, glancing over the room. "He was . . . an innocent."

She pressed her teeth together. She blinked away the water in her eyes. She never lost focus on where

Highlander sat several feet away from her bedside, far enough that she couldn't reach him but he could barely reach her.

"The feelings you have now," he continued, tracing the cast over her suspended leg, "The anger. The guilt. The grief. You should never forget them."

"Thanks," she said snidely. "I might have done just that."

He half chuckled and moved the bag to open it.

"Such feelings are important," he said.

She tried to see what he was reaching for without being too obvious. It was difficult while held by one leg in a hospital bed.

"With time you will forge them into a weapon."

He removed his hand from the bag and leaned to place something just inside the bed's rail. It was a contraption made of metal plates and leather straps. The shape, the size, and construction of the thing led Riley to believe it was meant to be worn on the arm.

"A weapon," the old man said, "against the wolf."